Single

Greatest

Threat

Atlantic City's Most Wanted #6

Charity Parkerson

Punk & Sissy Publications

COPYRIGHT

—Warning: This book is intended for readers over the age of 18. Some of my books contain allusions to past abuse and trauma.

CONTENTS

Introduction

Shaw did everything he could to destroy his personal life. He's doing his best to get back on track. Joesph doesn't believe a word of it.

For a long time, off and on, Shaw hooked up with another lawyer at his firm. It's over. After finally going too far, Joesph is totally out of his life. The move proved a universal point. He didn't know what he had until it was gone. Shaw will do anything to win back Joesph, even go to therapy and fix himself. He only has to convince Joesph this isn't another ploy. That sounds like a hopeless dream.

As dumb as it was, Joesph fell all the way in love with Shaw a long time ago. It's brought him nothing but heartache. Unfortunately, that love still exists, and he's not immune to Shaw's charm. He just has to stay strong. That's likely much harder than it sounds. He's hopeless and Shaw is the greatest threat to his sanity. Nothing good can come of giving romance a second chance. Maybe? He's in so much trouble.

Single Greatest Threat is the sixth book in Charity Parkerson's Atlantic City's Most Wanted series. These are sexy and sometimes dark stories where the richest and most dangerous men in Atlantic City meet their match. These are best enjoyed when read in order.

CHAPTER ONE

A BOX OF STUFF from his old desk sat on Joesph's lap as he wheeled his way inside Howe's Law offices. It had only been a month since he quit. Heaven knew he never intended to come back. But Shaw Howe Sr. had hired Joesph right out of law school and taught him the ropes. He had been a dream boss until the day he retired, leaving his son Shaw as the top attorney and in charge. Shaw Jr. was not his father. Joesph supposed that was a good thing, since they had been off and on friends with benefits for years. They were currently off. It was permanent. A move he had solidified when he had stormed out and quit. Now he was back. They still wouldn't be on again. Joesph was done with that bullshit. He'd been hurt enough.

Joesph flashed a smile at the receptionist and headed for his office. He genuinely hadn't intended to return. Only a call from Shaw Sr. had him here. Plus, a hefty raise and a promise his son would steer clear of Joesph. Oh, and Shaw wouldn't dump all his cases on Joesph—the way he had always done. That was another big one. Shaw had loved fucking Joesph in every way, including leaving him with more work than ten men could handle. Joesph was cautiously hopeful. If things went back to the way they used to be, he already had another job lined up. Truthfully, Joesph's worst fear was how he would feel when he saw Shaw. That might be the one thing he couldn't stand.

It was dumb. He was an idiot. While Shaw had been using him, Joesph fell in love. A tale as old as time. Thankfully, he had kept his feelings to himself. It was bad enough to love someone like Shaw—arrogant, successful, rich, and physically flawless. Joesph would be damned if he humiliated himself by admitting his feelings. He wasn't that pathetic.

His phone rang before he had half his box unpacked. Joesph checked the face. It was Dodge. A smile exploded across Joesph's face.

"Hello?" He set his cellphone on his desk and switched it to speakerphone so he could keep working.

"Hey. How are you?"

"I'm good. How are you?" He genuinely adored Dodge. They had only been friends for a few weeks, even though they had known each other for years. But after a long talk at a recent party, they realized how much they had in common. It was nice having a friend that was only that and let him feel free. Plus, Dodge was true blue sweet. He should be protected from the world.

"I'm good. Well, I'm kind of bored. Quest is the smart one, so he's handling the meeting with our accountant today. Something about payment for one of the latest games. Anyhow, he's gone, and

Salem had plans with Tarek, so I'm just kind of chilling."

Joesph hated when Dodge talked about himself as if he was dumb. He wasn't. Dodge was just a nice person in a cruel world. He didn't fit. It didn't help that Dodge was the picture shown in the dictionary under beautiful. Joesph had seen him literally stop traffic. Looks like that brought out predators and the worst of society.

"Today is my first day back at work."

Dodge huffed. "I told you not to go back. There's no reason to be around that guy when you have us." Joesph assumed "us" was Salem, Quest, and Dodge. Dodge didn't stop to expound. "We can afford to keep you."

A laugh burst from Joesph. He loved how Dodge talked about keeping a whole person like a pet. As one of the three beneficiaries of one of the world's richest men, Dodge had no real concept of money. "Sweetie, let me have my pride. Plus, what would I do all day anyhow? You have two fiancés. Your life is full. This is all I have."

"We could put you to work."

The pout in Dodge's voice had Joesph's affection growing. He knew Dodge only wanted him to be happy. But they needed to change the subject before Joesph cried. He didn't want to be here either. Not really. His bills didn't care about his pride. "So, what do you plan to do with the house all to yourself?"

Dodge immediately cheered. "I'd planned to see if you wanted to do something. Since you're working, I guess I'll have to settle with taking you to lunch."

"I'd love that." He really would. Joesph hadn't left the house before today in a couple of weeks. He hated doing things alone, and it wasn't easy being in a wheelchair. Joesph wasn't a full-time wheelchair user, so he wasn't an expert at navigating the world. Neither could he cane his way around for long before giving out. There weren't many people willing to do things with him, considering how much work it was. Dodge genuinely seemed to not mind.

"Yay! What time do you take lunch?"

Joesph automatically glanced toward the clock. He caught sight of Shaw heading inside his office. His brain stuttered before he remembered what he was doing. "Um. Anytime I want, really."

"Cool. How's eleven thirty? That way, I can make a noon reservation at Bigstock."

"Sounds great."

"Okay. Well, I guess I should let you get some work done."

Joesph's gaze refused to budge from the sight of Shaw moving around inside his office. It was obvious from the way he dressed and the stack of files he had, he'd spent the morning in court. Damn. He was just so fucking tall and sexy. Under his clothes was just... fuck. "Yeah. I guess I should do something." Like close his door.

A gorgeous chuckle rumbled through the line.

Shaw's head lifted, as if he heard the siren's call. Their gazes collided.

"I'll see you at eleven thirty."

Joesph tore his gaze away from the sexy dark green eyes that haunted him. "Yeah. See you then."

"Bye."

"Bye." Joesph tapped the face of his phone and went back to unpacking his things. He forced his gaze to stay locked on his task. Staring and longing was what had gotten him in this place to begin with. Dumbass heart. It never knew when to stop. Shaw didn't want him. Not really. Joesph was who Shaw had fucked when he got bored or hard up. Otherwise, he was always on the hunt for someone his equal. Joesph wasn't special. He was just easy. Not anymore.

"Hey."

Joesph's gaze shot toward the door. Shaw leaned against the frame, looking comfortable and way too lickable. "Hey."

"Dad said you'd be back today. I wasn't as sure."

Joesph focused on taking his plant back to the window. "Yeah. I showed."

"I'm glad you're here."

He bet. Shaw was probably sick of working and couldn't wait to dump everything on Joesph again. "Thanks." He turned.

Shaw immediately hid his expression.

Joesph's chest hurt. Coming back had been a bad idea. He couldn't handle Shaw acting like he wanted him again. They both knew it wasn't real.

Shaw straightened. "I should get back to work. It's good to see you."

Joesph dipped his chin. He wouldn't return the sentiment. They both already knew this was toxic. He already felt Shaw destroying his life again.

Those goddamn light blue eyes. They held so much hatred. Shaw forced himself to turn away and shut himself inside his office. Even as the door closed behind him, he fought the urge to turn around. He had fucked up so much and so hard. It seemed there was no going back. At least he had Joesph under the same roof again. Maybe he could keep at least that.

His phone rang as he sat behind his desk. Shaw didn't hesitate to snatch up the receiver. Only certain people could call his private line. "This is Shaw."

"Hey, son. How was court?"

"Hey, Dad. It was good. How are you?"

"Good. Good. Is Joesph back?"

Shaw knew damn well Kayla had called him already. She worked for his dad. Not him. His dad had made that apparent several times. She reported to him and no one else. If he dared reprimand her in any way, this practice could be taken away as easily as it had been given. It didn't feel like a gift.

"Yeah. I just spoke to him. His plant is back in the window."

"Why did you talk to him? I thought I made it clear you won't be doing the same shit as before. I'll be damned if that place is run by a tyrant."

Shaw rubbed his forehead. "I only said my good mornings, Dad. That's it."

A moment of silence met his words before his dad sighed. "I suppose that's good. That place shouldn't be an uncomfortable environment either."

For everyone except him.

"Got it."

"No need to get snarky."

"I'm not. Did you need something?"

Another uncomfortable bout of silence met his question. He had heard his tone and couldn't help it. Shaw was forty-five and his dad acted like he was twelve. It was exhausting and disheartening. He was a damn good lawyer. Shaw had more than paid his dues. In fact, he would go as far as to say he was a better attorney than his father had ever been. Not that it mattered. He would always live in his dad's shadow.

"Meet me at Bigstock in an hour."

Shaw's gaze moved toward the clock. It was ten in the morning. The place wasn't even open. He had to have made a reservation before today, and yet he just now called. That was typical of how little his dad respected Shaw's time. He could have had any plans at all and would be expected to drop them.

Shaw pinched the spot between his eyes. "Okay. I'll see you then."

"An hour."

"I heard you."

The phone disconnected in his ear, making Shaw sigh. He knew his dad cared about him. This was just who he was. It chafed, but he couldn't change him. With only thirty minutes to spare, since it would likely take him half an hour to get to the restaurant, Shaw checked his email. They were mostly junk with the smattering of inquiries about not hearing from Joesph. Until Joesph abandoned him a month ago, he hadn't realized how much he had turned the place over to him. Everyone called, texted, and emailed Joesph first. The only reason they contacted him was to find out why they couldn't reach Joesph. At one point, he supposed that was what he wanted. He kept Joesph tied to him while he did whatever he pleased. He liked knowing he had the control. It was only recently he realized exactly how miserable he was and how much his life had been on a downward spiral. He had heard people could be depressed and not know it. It had taken Joesph walking away to make him realize how bad things had gotten. Maybe it was a midlife crisis or maybe being completely unloved had finally caught up to him. Being alone showed its true form. It wasn't by choice. No one wanted him. Not for real. He knew that was his fault. Shaw was an asshole. He was stubborn and argumentative. Shaw was a good lawyer for a reason. But those personality traits didn't stay in the courtroom, and no one wanted that at home. He didn't know how to change.

With nothing left to do, Shaw headed out. He avoided looking at Joesph's closed office door and had Kayla hold his calls. Shaw climbed into his hundred-thousand-dollar car and drove slowly—like going to his judgment day—to the restaurant. He made it ten minutes early and stared at the door. As always, his dad showed up at exactly eleven. The man was as precise as the earth's rotation. Shaw put his emotions on lockdown and endured. The food was good. That was why the place was always busy. Shaw focused on his plate rather than the conversation. His dad rattled on about family Shaw never saw. Plans were made for his mom's birthday. Lunch only lasted an hour, and it was the longest hour of his life. Being with his dad drained the hell out of him. The guy was retired and still ran everything. For the millionth time, Shaw wondered what would happen if he walked away. He could buy a place in Malta. Live the slow life. Nothing was stopping him.

"Look. It's Joesph with J.D.'s son."

Shaw's gaze shot to the door at his dad's comment. Sure enough, someone held the door open as Dodge pushed Joesph's wheelchair inside. A pain sliced through Shaw at the sight of Joesph's bright smile. It was real. He was happy. Of course he was. He was with the most beautiful man on the planet. Dodge won everyone, including every man Shaw wanted.

"That's a good sign. Maybe he'll lure all that Rochester money our way."

His way. Shaw fought hard not to remind his dad that the practice belonged to Shaw now. It was his money. "Maybe." He knew it wasn't happening. Not only had J.D. been fiercely loyal to his attorney before he passed, but their firm also represented one of J.D.'s ex-wives. Dodge would never touch them.

The bill came and Shaw paid, even though lunch had been his dad's idea. He shouldn't have gotten distracted.

"Joesph!"

Shaw cringed as his dad shouted, as if they were in a barn and not in the middle of a nice restaurant.

He watched Joesph look their way and his smile turn fake. Shaw couldn't breathe. He had to get out of there before a panic attack hit. Therapy had been helping, but today wasn't a good day. Too much was happening at once. He was under his dad's microscope and Joesph was there with another man. It didn't matter that man was engaged. Joesph hated Shaw, and he had been Shaw's only real friend. Shaw had destroyed that. The room pressed in on him, choking him.

Shaw stood as Dodge pushed Joesph their way. The silverware rattled as he hit the table with his knees. His dad looked his way, irritated as always. Shaw fought a hysterical laugh at his thunderous expression, as if Shaw had embarrassed him and he hadn't been the one shouting moments earlier. His anxiety no longer cared about being polite. He mumbled his goodbyes and headed for the door without looking back. Shaw never met Joesph or Dodge's stare. He knew he looked like an ass, but it couldn't be helped. For months now, Shaw's mental health had been falling apart, and no one noticed or gave a damn. Sometimes he feared what he might do. It was time to get back to the office. He had to drown himself in work.

CHAPTER TWO

Joesph couldn't stop thinking about Shaw's expression as he had stormed from the restaurant. He knew the look of a drowning man. Joesph saw it all the time when he looked in the mirror since getting diagnosed with MS. Something was going on with Shaw. He felt that in his bones. Joesph hated he hadn't noticed before now. He had been trapped in his anger. Now he couldn't think about anything else.

He kept his office door open for the rest of the day. Shaw kept his closed until right before closing time. Joesph gathered his things when Shaw disappeared. Before he got the chance to head out, Shaw was back with coffee in hand. He sat behind his desk and got back to work. Stacks of files filled his desk. Joesph had no clue what he worked on, but it was obvious he intended to stay. That was so unlike Shaw that Joesph wheeled toward his office—like the fool he was.

"Hey. I'm headed out for the night."

Shaw looked up. His dark green eyes softened the moment they landed on Joesph. That was why he never stood a chance.

"Okay. Be careful going home. I'll see you tomorrow."

Joesph nodded. "What are you working on? Would you like some help?"

A wry smile touched Shaw's lips. "No, thank you. You've spent way too many long nights here over the years. It's my turn."

Joesph wheeled back and forth a hair, nervously rolling in place. "All right. I'll see you tomorrow." Joesph headed out with his mind all over the place. Why was Shaw suddenly acting this way? Was it a ploy? Why did he have so many files dragged out? Unfortunately, it wasn't a mystery quickly solved.

Several weeks passed. Each night, Joesph offered to stay, and Shaw declined. After the first two weeks, Joesph had secretly checked the security feed. Shaw never left his office until nearly midnight each night and was back at eight a.m. every day. He was like a man on a mission. More files appeared in his office until they stacked the walls. Six weeks in, Joesph broke.

"I'm headed out."

"Be careful going home." Shaw didn't look up from the paperwork he studied.

Joesph had deliberately waited until Kayla left. He wheeled his way deeper into Shaw's office. "Would you like some help?"

Shaw finally met his stare. "No. It's fine. Like I've said a hundred times, you've done your time. I've got this."

Joesph didn't back down. "Seriously. What are you working on? This office is out of control."

Shaw visibly hesitated. Finally, he sighed. "All right. Maybe you can tell me if I'm crazy." He held up the paper he read. Joesph wheeled to his side, leaning close so he could see. Fuck, he smelled good. It wasn't fair. Shaw pointed at a few numbers. "Okay. Look at these numbers."

Joesph nodded. "That seems a little high for our typical fee structure."

"Exactly." He dragged his laptop closer. "Now look at the digital copy. The numbers that hit the bank."

Joesph studied the two, comparing them. They weren't the same. The numbers deposited perfectly matched what they normally charged.

"I don't understand. Why are they different?"

"Right?" Shaw really got into things. "When I first spotted this a few months ago, I thought maybe it was a clerical error. I decided to dig out the client's file and go line by line to see if they were accidentally overcharged. They were, yet the right amount was deposited in the bank. So I called the client. The higher amount was paid. This led me down a rabbit hole." He swept his arm wide. "Nearly every file has been the same. At this point, I'm just adding up the overcharge amount and making a list of how much is owed to each client." He hesitated again. "I need a full total to prosecute Kayla."

Joesph's lips parted in surprise. He didn't know what to say. "Kayla? Are you sure? She's been here forever."

Shaw nodded and picked up a file that had been singled out from the rest. "This is the oldest one I've found. The over-charge fees are smaller than the rest and they grew from there. This is from a year after she started working here."

Joesph was dumbfounded. Shaw was right. The only person it could be was Kayla. While they had several parale-gals and a dedicated accountant, Kayla handled billing and payments. She made their deposits and kept the paperwork for the accountant. Literally, no one else touched any of that.

"What do you need me to do?"

Shaw's sweet smile stole Joesph's breath. He didn't see this real and kind version of Shaw often. It was the version he loved. "Go home. I genuinely don't want you to feel the way you did before you quit. Maybe I'm a slow learner, but I got it. You deserve much better than you've ever gotten from me."

"I never meant for you to take on everything. All I wanted was your help. You're helping now. Let me help you."

"I started counseling."

Nothing could have shocked Joesph more than that confession.

Shaw didn't stop. "The night you told me you didn't want me in your life anymore, I had a huge revelation that won't surprise you at all. I'm the problem."

Joesph might have laughed if this didn't seem so important to Shaw.

Thankfully, Shaw kept going and didn't expect him to confirm or deny because, yeah, Shaw was the problem.

"I'm cold and narcissistic. My only thoughts are about my happiness. I refused to help around here once Dad left. In my mind, I had proven myself and earned my freedom. But you're the only opinion I've ever cared about, and you said you were done." He shrugged, looking uncomfortable now that his confession was out there. "So, I'm working on me. Though I'm not sure if it's actually working."

A smile pulled at the corners of Joesph's mouth. He was so proud of Shaw. "It is. The old you would've never admitted any of that to yourself, much less to me."

For a moment, that felt way too personal. Shaw held his stare. "I miss you."

Damn. He really was screwed. "I miss you too."

Shaw nodded and straightened in his chair. He heard Shaw's back pop. Shaw rubbed the back of his neck. "You should head home. I've already kept you late. Thanks for validating that I'm not insane."

Joesph chuckled and shook his head. He wheeled his chair backward. "Don't over-work yourself too much. Kayla's proba-bly getting suspicious of all these files."

Shaw nodded. He waited until Joesph made it to the door to speak again. "Hey."

Joesph glanced over his shoulder.

Shaw looked uncomfortable. "Can I take you to dinner?"

Fuck. His heart wouldn't let him say no. "I'd like that." Joesph knew he was an idiot. He didn't doubt Shaw would make him regret this. There was only one way to find out. Joesph had to fling himself against the wall again and hope he didn't break.

Shaw was a little proud of the way he managed to move at a normal pace. He wanted to jump from his desk and rush to the door. Instead, he stood and gathered his phone. He stuffed it in his pocket before locking his office door and pulling it closed behind him.

"Come on." He took control of Joesph's wheelchair. It was a move he knew Joesph equally appreciated and hated.

As expected, Joesph argued. "You don't have to push me. I got it."

Shaw didn't stop. "Look, I know you hate feeling like a burden, but I've never seen this that way. I love spending time with you and taking care of you. You're my best friend. I know I should've said that a long time ago, so I get it's my fault you don't want my help."

Joesph didn't respond, but he stopped arguing. Shaw took what he could get. Joesph set the alarm and then they backed out the door. He handed Joesph his keys so he could lock the office. Working together, Joesph was in his passenger seat and Shaw had the wheelchair stuffed in his trunk in no time. The satisfaction Shaw felt once he was on the road with Joesph trapped was off the charts. There was no way Joesph knew how much Shaw missed him and wanted him here.

"Where would you like to go?"

Joesph laughed. "I have no idea. You asked me."

Shaw realized he was smiling and couldn't stop. "That's right. You're the guest. You should choose."

A humming sound came from Joesph's side of the car that nearly made Shaw steer off the road so he could jump Joesph. He hadn't known a person could miss someone so badly. Shaw doubted Joesph would ever let Shaw touch him again. That was okay. He would rather have some of him than none of him.

"Honestly, I'm sick of every restaurant imaginable. It's crazy to cook for just me, so I've gotten bad about picking up take-out on the way home every night."

"It's less mess and shopping."

"Exactly." He heard the commiseration in Joesph's voice. "It's a hell of a lot easier for me to get in the house too. If I don't have groceries delivered, which is getting crazy expensive, it's an exhausting hundred trips between the car and the house, wheeling in two bags at a time... if I'm lucky. Then I'm so tired afterward, I don't want to cook anything, which is also such a goddamn chore. Everything is, really."

Shaw heard the sadness in Joesph's voice, but hope like he never expected filled Shaw's chest. Joesph didn't talk to other people like this. He pretended to be unbothered by how life had changed for him. They had been friends before Joesph's life had changed. Shaw had watched Joesph go from being an active guy with zero health issues to barely being able to crawl from bed seemingly overnight. He was the perfect example of how a person could do everything right for their health and still get struck down. It was humbling and terrifying the way it could happen to anyone. He watched Joesph go through the stages of grief, mourning the loss of his old self, over and over again. Shaw was the worst fucking human on earth, because he had known all of that, and he had used Joesph anyhow. Every minute. As if Joesph's life was flawless and Shaw's to take, Shaw had treated him worse than a homeless person he passed on the street. At least a homeless person would have been left no worse by Shaw pretending they didn't exist. He was a terrible person who didn't deserve Joesph, but he would.

Once the thought hit, it grew. He would. Shaw could start now. He could start over. "You know what? I have an idea." Shaw changed lanes and headed for the closest grocery store to Joesph's place. Fresh life filled his lungs. Shaw didn't have to be the person he hated so badly. He didn't have to be the guy who had come so close to taking his own life.

His throat swelled without warning. The saddest part was, no one knew, because he had no one. Not really. Joesph would have been there for him, despite his own problems, but Shaw had already ruined them before he had ended up spending a week doing inpatient treatment. He hadn't told a soul. Shaw had been his usual selfish and cocky self, playing the role as he took another vacation. Except he had driven four hours away and checked himself into a "spa" for the rich. He wasn't sure it helped. The meds made some difference, but—a lot of days—Shaw still barely hung on.

With his thoughts spiraling, he tossed himself into being Joesph's friend—the way he should have done a long time ago. He pulled into the grocery store parking lot.

Joesph laughed. It was a nervous sound. "We're not going pity shopping, are we?"

Shaw snorted as he put the car in park. "When have I ever done anything out of pity?" He didn't wait for an answer. Shaw wasn't in the right headspace to hear to

Joesph agree. He climbed from the car and grabbed Joesph's wheelchair. Shaw explained as Joesph pushed his way from the car, holding on and steadying himself until he was safely seated again in the chair. "I have a proposal for you." Shaw headed for the door. He stopped by a stack of hand baskets. "Grab a basket."

Joesph did so without arguing.

Shaw kept talking. His mood lifted by the second. "Let's grab stuff for a few nights' worth of dinners. I'll buy and help cook the rest of the week, and we can get a break from takeout."

"How is that a deal? That's you doing everything."

The laughter in Joesph's voice kept Shaw smiling. He hadn't been this happy in a long time. "Of course it's a deal. We're using your kitchen, your electricity, and you'll be helping. Not to mention, I get your time. I know how precious that is, considering how little I deserve it."

Joesph didn't respond, but he didn't argue, so Shaw started walking down aisles. He hadn't eaten a home-cooked meal in forever. Shaw actually loved to cook, but it was ridiculous to do so for just one person. Plus, it was lonely as hell. Nothing highlighted how empty his life was quite like sitting down for a meal alone. It was a hell of a lot easier to grab something and eat while poring over work. His throat suddenly swelled again, stealing the happiness he had just regained. He couldn't even imagine how Joesph felt each night, eating alone. Fuck. He had left Joesph isolated. Shaw didn't deserve his time.

"You're my best friend too."

At Joesph's sudden, quietly spoken confession, Shaw nearly bent at the waist and sucked air. It was that hard of a punch to the chest. He stopped at the meat section and stared at the selection, seeing nothing. His hands moved from the chair to Joesph's shoulders without thinking. Once he touched Joesph, he couldn't stop. Shaw massaged.

To cover the way he couldn't tear his hands away, he fell back on faked charm. "What should we eat, sexy? I'm game for anything, but it should probably be something simple tonight since it's already getting late."

"How about tacos?"

Damn. He hadn't had tacos in forever. "We should do the full spread. Like a taco bar." Shaw got into the spirit. "I'll send

Kylie to your place tomorrow to clean up the mess."

To his surprise, Joesph didn't argue about Shaw's cleaning lady coming to his house. "Grab a couple of steaks. If we leave the office on time tomorrow, we can fire up the grill."

Shaw put the things they needed in the basket. "Leave on time? I'm the boss. Let's leave an hour early."

Joesph's smile was everything. His light blue eyes sparkled with happiness. Shaw had to tear his gaze away. He still remembered exactly how soft Joesph's light brown hair felt when Shaw held on to it as Joesph bobbed on his dick. Shaw shoved the thoughts from his mind. They were just friends now. He couldn't let his brain go there. Joesph had always been the single greatest threat to his heart. That was why Shaw had always run like hell from the guy. Shaw didn't want to run anymore and now it was too late. He had ruined any shot of Joesph loving him. They could be friends again, though. Shaw would take it. He knew he didn't deserve a damn thing.

CHAPTER THREE

BY THE TIME THEY finished shopping, there was so much shit in Joesph's lap, he could barely hold it all. Shaw had definitely grabbed a lot more brand-name, high-quality things than Joesph ever would have. That was how Joesph comforted himself. If Shaw stopped talking to him again after Joesph refused to fuck him tonight, then at least Joesph had gotten groceries. He recognized that was a shitty way to look at things, but Shaw had been a crappy friend. Joesph doubted he could trust this sudden change. Shaw had always had an amazing streak that came and went. He was mental destruction on two legs. Joesph didn't have anything left to give.

Life at home was a combination of easier and harder. He knew that didn't make sense to anyone who didn't live it. At home, he could move around a little freer. He felt safer about falling, so he used a combination of cane and walker, swapping between the two as needed. There just wasn't enough space in his house to use his wheelchair and his walker was one of those with the seat that also wouldn't fit through every space. It was a bit freeing to feel like he could walk around some, but it was exhausting. Likely he was more in the way than not as he pushed his walker around in Shaw's wake, sitting each time they stopped. Truthfully, he was useless, but he didn't leave Shaw's side while Shaw cooked and chopped vegetables.

Shaw opened the fridge and grabbed a bottle of water. As he closed the door, he eyed the line of appointment cards sticking from behind magnets.

He twisted the cap from his bottle. "How is everything going with your treatment?"

Joesph hated talking about his health, but it was Shaw. "Tedious. It feels like I'm always at the doctor, yet nothing changes. I'm just shoveling money their way so I can get my zillion scripts refilled every month. My mom always wants to know what I found out at every appointment, like anything ever changes. The answer is nothing. They stare at that little lap-top thing, ask the same questions, get the same answers, and then tell me they'll see me in three months. I'm just another number to them."

Shaw held his stare as he spoke. Joesph couldn't explain it. He never had been able to say what it was about Shaw. Joesph told things to him he didn't admit to anyone else. Shaw asked the same questions everyone did, but Joesph's answers were real with Shaw. That was why Joesph couldn't quit him. He didn't feel this way with anyone else.

"I know it has to be frustrating."

Joesph's hands rose and fell. "It is what it is."

A sweet and sexy smile touched Shaw's lips. "I know life hasn't given you any other choice, but you're still the strongest person I know." He went back to cooking.

Joesph's gaze moved down Shaw's body. It was beyond his control. They were back to feeling like a couple again and Joesph hated himself for that, but fuck. Shaw was tall and perfectly formed. He had a tight, round ass that begged to be squeezed and bitten. Joesph chewed the side of his nail to keep his hand from reaching out. He knew exactly what was beneath those expensive dress pants. His tie was gone, and his shirtsleeves were rolled up to his elbows. Shaw's feet were bare. God. He hated feet, but Shaw's were sexy. How fucked up was that? It got worse. He had been the one to suggest Shaw take off his socks so they didn't get wet when they inevitably splashed water all over the floor. Joesph had done it for just this reason, so he could look at his feet. Shaw had him fucked up. Always had. He was pathetic. Joesph was kind of glad he didn't have the energy to jump him. At least he wouldn't make too big of a fool of himself.

Then they were squeezed in together at Joesph's tiny kitchen table and all Joesph smelled was Shaw. Even the delicious scent of tacos couldn't drown out the cologne that Joesph knew so well. Worse, he knew that scent mixed with sex, and Joesph was a goddamn mess of memories and need. He ate, but that wasn't what he truly wanted. His body craved so much more than food. Life never took mercy on him. Tonight didn't look to be any different.

Being with Joesph was such a mixture of heaven and hell. No one looked at him the way Joesph did. Even once they had cleaned their plates and the kitchen, Shaw couldn't make himself leave. Thankfully, Joesph didn't seem to be in any hurry to kick him out.

"Have you seen the latest season of *Out*?"

Shaw followed Joesph to the living room. "No. You're the only person I watch TV with. I mean, I don't bother turning on the TV. Have I missed anything good?"

Joesph shrugged. "I haven't watched past the last episode we saw together."

Awesome. The excuse he needed. "You want to finish it?"

"Yeah, that's why I brought it up."

"Cool." Shaw picked his usual spot on the small loveseat and kicked up the footrest.

Joesph joined him and matched his pose before turning on the TV. He pulled up their show from whatever streaming service it was on. Shaw had no idea which. He had been completely serious. Without Joesph, his life was silent.

Shaw's gaze scanned the room to keep from staring at Joesph. Joesph's place was tiny. Sometimes he forgot the huge disparity between their lifestyles. While Shaw's father paid Joesph well, it was nothing compared to what the law office provided for Shaw. Plus, Shaw had grown up wealthy and gotten a lion's share of his grandparents' money when they had passed... from both sides. Even though Joesph would likely argue, Joesph missed nothing by not having as much. Fake people. Fake friends. Greedy eyes and hands. That had been Shaw's entire life. That was all Joesph missed. Joesph was real. He wasn't like those people. Still, Shaw hated the way Joesph struggled. His medical bills sucked him dry. The smaller place was likely easier for him to manage, though. Shaw's gaze automatically slid Joesph's way again. His hair was a mess. Shaw wanted to touch him so fucking badly. The craving was near to being crippling. He forced himself to focus on the show.

It had been a while since he watched the series, so it took all his concentration to catch up. The first episode ended. Shaw glanced Joesph's way when he didn't immediately skip the intro of the next episode. He was asleep. A smile tugged at Shaw's lips. He carefully slipped the remote from Joesph's side of the couch and turned off the TV. Then he went back to staring at Joesph, studying his every line. He still remembered the first time Joesph called him out for staring. He'd been wearing a white shirt that day un-buttoned at the collar. Everything about him looked sexy.

Shaw was fascinated by Joesph's baby blue eyes and the smattering of freckles across the bridge of his nose. His light brown hair brushed the collar of his shirt and curled at the ends, making Shaw want to touch it. When he smiled... god-damn. The world stopped spinning. He couldn't stop staring at those perfect lips.

The way they curved into the most devilish of smirks always took his breath. Shaw had no idea why he couldn't shake the guy. He just wanted him.

Those fuckable lips took on the slightest of smiles while Shaw watched. "You're staring at me."

"I'm not."

At his blatant lie, Joesph looked up from his paperwork. He leaned his chair back, matching Shaw's relaxed pose. "You're bored."

He wasn't. Not in the least. Shaw could sit like this for the rest of his life. That thought stopped him cold. He didn't want anyone forever. Shaw had no idea why he had forgotten that. The last thing he wanted was to hurt Joesph by making promises he couldn't keep. They were friends. A whimper rang through his head. God, he ached for him.

"This case is tedious." It was all Shaw could think to say in the face of Joesph's open interrogation.

Joesph flipped his file closed and sat forward. His eyes stayed locked on Shaw, making Shaw feel like he slowly fell into them. "Then let's do something else. All this can wait for one night. We could go to dinner, dancing, or even back to my place to watch TV. Anything is better than this. What do you want to do?"

"You." No one was more shocked than Shaw. He had not meant to say that. Joesph made him weak. Damnit. He had to fix things. Shaw laughed. It was an uncomfortable sound. "Well, that's a sexual

harassment suit waiting to happen. Sorry."

Joesph didn't laugh or even smile. He simply held Shaw's stare. "Were you serious?"

He didn't know how to respond. Shaw didn't want to lie and miss his shot. He equally didn't want that harassment suit he'd mentioned. But the longer he held Joesph's stare, the more the heat built between them. Shaw was hard as fuck and Joesph hadn't done a thing but look into his eyes. It hit Shaw. He saw Shaw. It was pointless to deny it. Joesph would know if he lied.

"Yeah. I'm serious."

Joesph stood and circled the war room table, where they had been silently working for hours.

Shaw watched every step with his breath held. He didn't know what Joesph would do. His expression gave nothing away. Maybe he'd punch Shaw. It wasn't like Shaw didn't deserve it.

"Let's go, then."

Shaw shot to his feet so fast, he nearly upset the table. No way would he give Joesph time to take it back. He couldn't do an uncomfortable car ride where they didn't acknowledge what Joesph had just agreed to do. Shaw snagged Joesph before he got away. They met each other's gaze, and something snapped inside Shaw. His mouth came down hard on Joesph's. When their tongues met and Joesph came back at him with matched desperation, Shaw glimpsed insanity. The need won. He swiped the stack of files from the table and sat Joesph where they had been. His mouth moved to Joesph's neck as he tried his ass off to get Joesph out of his shirt. He would fuck Joesph right here. Damn the consequences. Joesph was worth the risk of losing everything.

A sexy chuckle caressed his ears. "You know someone will have to pick that up tomorrow."

Shaw changed directions, needing to taste the other side of Joesph's neck to see if it was just as delicious. It was. "So."

Another of those goddamn toe-curling chuckles vibrated against his lips as he kissed his way lower. "So, that someone is me."

"It won't be." Joesph sounded way too coherent.

Shaw had to fix that. Joesph sounded exactly like a man who needed his dick sucked. He should get started on that.

Shaw still saw that same guy who sent him spiraling out of control and felt that same passion. Nothing had changed except the smudges beneath Joesph's eyes. Shaw's brow furrowed. Joesph claimed there was nothing new to tell about his health, but he looked exhausted. Shaw checked the time. It likely wasn't too late yet. He snagged the throw blanket from the back of the couch and covered Joesph. With that out of the way, he grabbed his phone and scrolled through his contacts until he found Joesph's mom's number. Unless something had changed, Haven didn't usually go to bed before eleven. For an older lady, she was still a night owl. Even though he knew he had no right, Shaw didn't hesitate to text her.

Shaw: *Hey, beautiful lady. Are you still breaking hearts?*

There. He hit send. Shaw hadn't led with being nosey. To his delight, three little dots danced, showing she worked on a response.

Haven: *Shaw! Holy shit, boy. Where have you been?*

Shaw: *A mental institution. Can I ask about Joesph?*

Haven: *HA! Just skimming over that comment. I know you won't tell me anything anyhow. Ask away. Is he not talking to you or something?*

CHARITY PARKERSON

Oddly, Shaw didn't hesitate to say his every thought to Haven. She was just one of those people. Zero judgment.

Shaw: *It was a suicide thing. Nothing special. Joesph's actually asleep on the couch next to me. That's why I asked. He looks a little more worn down than what matches his health updates.*

Haven: *Sigh. I see. Ever the prideful one. I keep hoping you two will fall madly in love and you'll make his life easier. A mother can dream. He's relapsed. This isn't a normal flare-up. He ended up hospitalized a couple of months ago and it hasn't let up since. They're trying new treatments, but the pain has been crippling. I'm scared as hell of what all this means.*

Goddamn it. Haven was right. Shaw needed to take care of him. Joesph was too stubborn and good at hiding his symptoms.

Shaw: *Thank you for letting me know. I can't help if he won't talk to me. Knowledge is power. I've got him.*

Haven: *I'm glad to hear it. You know I love you, but these old bones need rest. Drag Joesph to see me. He's been avoiding everyone.*

Not everyone. Joesph still had lunch dates with Dodge. Shaw tried not to get jealous, but damn. He wanted to be the only man in Joesph's life.

Shaw: *I'll get him there. Love you too. Dream of me.*

A laugh escaped Shaw as he hit send. Haven was so much fun. She was nothing like anyone in Shaw's family. He envied Joesph. Not everyone got the love Joesph did. Shaw's gaze slid back Joesph's way. He wanted to ask why Joesph fought so hard to hide his pain, but Shaw already knew. Joesph couldn't count on Shaw and likely would die before showing Shaw an ounce of weakness. It didn't matter. Joesph didn't have to ask. Shaw needed to focus on something other than himself and Joesph needed Shaw. It was a win-win. Joesph would see.

CHAPTER FOUR

FOR FIVE MINUTES, JOESPH reveled in the sweetness of waking up covered up. Shaw had obviously taken care of him before leaving. His phone had been on charge and everything. Then reality had set in. His car was back at the office and his wheelchair was in the trunk of Shaw's car. Joesph got ready and pulled out his phone to hire an Uber. The doorbell rang, saving him. A smile exploded across Joesph's face when he spotted Shaw through the peephole. He tried tempering his reaction before opening the door.

Shaw didn't wait for a hello. "Good. You're still here. I worried you'd try to find another way to work without your chair since I'm running behind." He handed Joesph the Styrofoam container he held. "I know you didn't eat. You know you get flare-ups when you skip meals."

Joesph bit his bottom lip and turned to grab his cane. Before he could fumble too much, Shaw took his keys from him and locked the house.

"Thank you."

Shaw tucked the keys in his pocket. "Of course. Come on."

Joesph fought for his life not to smile like an idiot. Two days in a row, he got the good Shaw. His heart couldn't take it. It was dumb to be hopeful, even though his brain knew this was temporary, that love still existed...on his end.

Shaw opened the passenger side door for Joesph, helping him get settled. When the door closed, Joesph let himself have a second of grinning before Shaw was behind the wheel.

Shaw pointed at the cup holders between them. "The coffee in front is yours."

"Thank you." It was all Joesph could think to say. He sipped the drink while the car was still parked and there was no risk of spilling it. The coffee was doctored perfectly because, of course, it was.

Shaw backed from the driveway. When they were on their way, he motioned toward the food sitting on Joesph's lap. "Eat."

"I don't want to eat in your car. It's too nice."

An annoyed look shot his way. "Your health is more important than my leather seats."

Memories slammed into Joesph, making him glad he was already sitting.

"You look tired today."

Joesph winced. "Thanks for that." That was just what he needed on top of feeling sick.

"Let me get you something to eat. You don't look after your health anymore the

way you should." Shaw looked twice as sexy when he showed his caring heart.

Joesph wished like hell he felt good enough to seduce him. He nearly whimpered at the thought. That body... yum. "I'm good. I think I'm just coming down with something."

"Nope. You're not good. Don't move. I'll be right back."

Joesph shook his head. He wished Shaw would stop pointing out how terrible he looked. With a sigh, he went back to searching the law books on his desk for specific case numbers.

Shaw was back in no time. At least he thought Shaw had been quick, except he held a bag full of hot food from a restaurant down the street. Joesph looked at his book. He was still reading the same page. It was like he had lost time.

Shaw rearranged the things on Joesph's desk so he could set out their meal. "I figured I'd join you."

His adorable guilty expression had Joesph feeling slightly better. "Good. I hate eating alone."

"I know." Shaw flashed him one of those irresistible smiles that kept Joesph awake at night. "Damnit."

"What?" Damn. Even the aggravated line between Shaw's brows was sexy.

"I forgot drinks."

"No problem. I'll grab a couple from the break room." Joesph pushed to his feet. His head spun. He took one step and was on

the floor with his head on Shaw's lap with no clue how he got there.

"Are you okay? Holy shit, Joesph. You scared the hell out of me. Talk to me."

Joesph still had no idea how he ended up on the floor. For pride's sake, he wanted to claim he was fine. But this wasn't the first time this had happened, and Joesph felt out of control. There was something wrong with him and it was starting to scare him. "I don't know what's wrong with me." Even Joesph heard the sheer terror in his voice.

Shaw ran his fingers through Joesph's hair. "Don't worry." He kissed Joesph's forehead. "I'll take care of you. You're not alone. Okay? I'll always take care of you."

Fuck. It would happen. Joesph would let Shaw wreck him again. He practically heard the clock ticking on the hammer fall. Joesph flipped open the lid on his food container. The delicious scent of a southwestern omelet smacked him in the face. "Oh, damn. This is that good one from Millie's Cafe."

"Of course. It's your favorite. I wouldn't buy you something you won't eat." Shaw was so matter-of-fact—like Joesph should know he could trust him.

Joesph grabbed the plastic fork waiting inside and dug in. It was still warm and so delicious. He tried not to hum with happiness. Joesph didn't normally eat breakfast. He preferred to sleep in as late as possible. The exhaustion of being chronically ill was real and constant. His life revolved around what his body could do and handle now. That was why he no longer had many friends.

"Thanks again. This is perfect." He had to focus on something other than his thoughts. Those were a downward spiral.

"It's no big deal. Millie's is between your house and mine."

Joesph had been so focused on his food, he hadn't realized they weren't heading toward the office. "Where are we going?"

"I closed the office today so we can take care of some things."

Irritation struck. Here they went with Shaw being Shaw, acting like the office just ran on magic. "I have appointments with clients today."

Shaw glanced his way. "Not anymore. I rescheduled everything for later this week. We have something else to take care of today. Well, I do." Shaw hesitated. "And I really don't want to do it alone."

There was something in Shaw's voice. "What's up?"

"It's time to talk to Dad about Kayla. I know the office is mine, but really, it isn't."

Yeah. Joesph knew that. Shaw Sr. would never relinquish full control.

Shaw's knuckles turned white on the steering wheel, proving how that constant meddling and lecturing bothered him. "While I could press charges without Dad onboard, who knows what he would do if he feels like I've gone around him?" He tossed Joesph a look. "Really. I don't want to do this alone."

"Okay." He wouldn't make Shaw beg. They both knew how Shaw's dad could be. He liked Joesph, but that was only because Joesph had let them use him eighteen hours a day for years. They were probably the reason he was sick. Shaw was the best fucking lawyer Joesph had ever seen in his life. His IQ and ability to charm a jury were off the charts. He was amazing. Yet Shaw would never be good enough for his dad. Joesph couldn't imagine.

"You know I've got your back."

At his statement, Shaw flashed him a blinding smile that stole Joesph's breath.

Joesph focused on his food to protect his sanity. The omelet was gone before Joesph realized it. He drank his coffee. It was halfway gone before the truth struck him. They had always been comfortable. Sitting in silence with Shaw was peaceful. He liked it. Joesph supposed he had always known he liked Shaw's company even when they did nothing at all, but he had never looked too closely. His relationship with Shaw was a raw spot he tried not to pick at. Shaw Sr's house came into view, giving Joesph something else to focus on. The stucco house sat on a hill overlooking the ocean. It wasn't as big or as nice as where Dodge lived, but still way more than Joesph would ever have. Not that he could navigate the stairs anyhow.

"You closed the office for the entire day for this. Do you expect your dad will be difficult?"

Shaw chuckled as he steered into the driveway. "Dad is always difficult. But in this case, I didn't want Kayla getting arrested at the office with clients watching. Plus, I have no idea how I'll replace her. Honestly, if she had just asked for more money, I probably would've given it to her just so I wouldn't have to find someone new. It's the betrayal I can't stomach."

Joesph nodded. That would matter a great deal to Shaw. While Shaw had stomped on Joesph's heart, he had never lied. He never claimed they were more than friends or made promises. Shaw's entire business model was built on integrity. Their office kept some of the biggest criminals on the east coast out of prison. Shaw had to be loyal to hold on to that clientele.

"We'll go in through the garage to avoid the front steps."

Joesph nodded. He planned to cane his way around, but Shaw was out of the car and dragging out Joesph's wheelchair before Joesph had time to offer to be less of a burden. Once Joesph was settled, he twisted and met Shaw's stare. "You've got this. I saw the evidence too. If you need me to jump in, just let me know."

A sad-looking smile touched Shaw's lips. "Okay."

Joesph hated the way Shaw obviously dreaded seeing his own father. He would give anything to see his again. Joesph got it, though. Their dads were nothing alike. They passed two workers on the way inside. One looked to be doing laundry. The other was kitchen staff. It was hard for Joesph to wrap his mind around growing up this way. Shaw never hesitated to cook or clean. Joesph had no clue how Shaw had turned out the way he had. While the guy was still spoiled, he didn't expect others to do everything for him. Joesph wondered if he would ever do anything for himself if he had been raised in the same wealth. Maybe he would have turned out to be a piece of shit. At least he would be a shitty person without a hundred thousand dollars in college loans and almost as much in medical bills. Joesph took a breath. He couldn't think about that.

They found Shaw Sr. in the dining room. He looked surprised to see them. It was obvious Shaw hadn't called ahead. "What are you doing here? Who's at the office?"

Joesph stayed silent. He let Shaw handle everything.

"I closed for the day so we could come and discuss something with you."

Senior looked between them. "I can't believe you green-lit this laziness, Joesph. Now Shaw is always useless, but you've never let me down."

Fuck. The rage was real. Shaw looked closed, but unfazed. Thankfully, Shaw didn't give Joesph time to speak and ruin his life. "Yes. I'm the disappointment. Anyhow, I found something unfortunate while going through some paperwork." He pulled out a chair and sat. "It seems Kayla has been skimming off every transaction for years. I haven't made it through every file yet and it's already up to nearly six figures."

Senior's dark green eyes—so much like his son's—slid from Shaw to Joesph and back again. "Joesph, please wait in the kitchen."

Joesph didn't hesitate to back his chair away and find his way to the kitchen. The tone had left no room for argument, but Joesph pretended to struggle a bit so Shaw could have time to stop him if he wanted Joesph to stay. Shaw didn't speak up, so Joesph left them alone.

He wheeled his way inside the kitchen and was immediately met with overly helpful staff. They offered coffee and homemade donuts, but Joesph didn't have time to answer before Shaw was there. His expression was colder than Joesph had ever seen. He took control of Joesph's chair before Joesph had time to ask a single thing. Joesph let it happen. He had questions, but he kept his mouth shut until they were a good five miles from Shaw's dad's house. Joesph had never seen Shaw so thunderous.

"I'm guessing that didn't go well."

Shaw had one hand on the wheel and the other propping up his head. His elbow was braced on the door. He looked ready to blow. "You could say that."

Joesph tried to be quiet. Silence wasn't quite so comfortable anymore. "Okay. Well. I'm here whenever you want to talk."

Shaw suddenly veered off the road and into the parking lot of a closed night club. He put the car in park. "It seems my dad has always known about Kayla."

That one threw Joesph. "Okay. What?"

Shaw looked his way. Joesph saw the fire inside that Shaw tried to keep at bay.

"She takes money. He turns a blind eye. She doesn't tell my mom about their affair."

Holy hell. Joesph was flabbergasted. He was beyond speechless. All he could do was stare at Shaw and try his damnedest to process. Shaw's openly downward spiral was what rescued Joesph. He had to save him. "Tell me what to do. How can I help? Let's fix it." Joesph was just that guy. They knew the problem now. He could help Shaw face it head on.

Shaw's hands rose and fell. "I just—"

Joesph got it. "Okay. Get out and let me drive."

He watched Shaw's throat work as he swallowed. "I don't know where to go."

Shaw's phone rang. "Dad" showed on the car's system screen. Shaw angrily hit reject and then turned off his phone. Joesph's phone rang.

He dug out his phone and stared at Shaw Sr's name. Joesph didn't know what to do. He wasn't Shaw. Joesph couldn't ignore his boss.

Shaw grabbed the phone from his hand and rejected the call before turning off Joesph's phone. He climbed from the vehicle and circled the car. They swapped sides. As Joesph pulled back into traffic, he had no clue where he was headed or if he would still have a job when the day was done. He would be here for Shaw, though. It seemed the time had finally come to let Shaw completely destroy him.

The way Shaw's mind swirled terrified him. He was so angry and hurt, he didn't know where to start. They couldn't go home. His dad had to know Shaw might choose to tell his mom everything. Since he couldn't reach either of them by phone, Shaw imagined he would try their houses next. Thankfully, Joesph obviously had the same realization. He seemed to drive around town aimlessly.

An old idea took root and grew. Shaw just needed time and space to figure out a solid plan and find his footing before presenting it to Joesph. "How do you feel about Aspen?"

Joesph shot him an odd look. "What? Why? You know I'm too poor to have ever been to Aspen. What would I do there? It's not like I can ski."

Damn. He had sounded terrible. "Yeah. Sorry. I'm just trying to think of somewhere to go so I can have a few days to think and figure this out."

Shaw watched Joesph's shoulders relax. "Oh. We have to work tomorrow."

He really didn't want to point out the obvious. "I just rejected my dad's call to you. We maybe don't have to work tomorrow." Joesph's shoulders fell a little more. Guilt ate at him. Shaw couldn't fail him. "Don't worry. I know it's asking a lot, considering how big of a fuck-up I am, but can you just trust me this one time? I promise I'll make sure you're fine. Okay?"

Joesph cast a quick glance his way. That was all it took to see the loyalty. "I'm always on your side. Don't worry about me. I already had another job lined up before I came back. It's less money, but whatever."

Goddamn it. Joesph had already accepted Shaw would ruin him and had a backup plan. He didn't get a chance to reassure him again.

"Your dad knows you. If you run away to any of your usual spots, he'll just show up there. Why don't we go stay with my mom? Of course, I need to grab my meds. We can't avoid going to my place. Just leave me somewhere and I'll take a cab home. You can go wherever you want."

"No. We've probably got a couple of hours before he comes after me. He's too used to me falling in line. There's no reason for him to think I won't this time too. Let's be quick. Your place first. I'll run in and grab everything. Then we'll hit my place. Staying with your mom sounds great. My dad would never think of her. He's used to parents being like him."

Joesph reached over and took his hand. He squeezed. Once Shaw had him, he refused to let go. Maybe it was shitty to use a situation like this, but he couldn't stop. Joesph willingly touched him. He needed that.

Joesph headed for his place, rattling off a list of what he would need. It got a little extensive. When he hit a list of toiletries, Shaw cut in. "Stick with your meds and clothes. I'll grab all the toiletries from my place. There's no sense in having two sets for one bathroom."

Joesph bit his bottom lip.

Shaw wished he hadn't pointed out that detail. Haven's house was small. Two bedrooms and two bathrooms. One bathroom was in her room. They would have to sleep together in the spare bedroom and share the bathroom. He held his breath, expecting Joesph would take it back.

Joesph surprised him. "Yeah. That makes the most sense, especially since your stuff is way better than mine."

Shaw wanted to growl. It was like Joesph only thought about their differences now. Almost like he constantly listed the ways Shaw was better in his head, and he couldn't see Shaw was actually less. Shaw didn't know how to say any of that.

Then words just fell out. "I don't know. Maybe I should grab your stuff instead. You always smell amazing. Sometimes I hold my breath when you're close, so I don't forget we're friends." Even Shaw heard the longing in his voice. He wouldn't take it back.

Joesph didn't respond. He kept his gaze locked on the road like his life depended on it, but he still didn't take back his hand. Shaw would take what he could get.

CHAPTER FIVE

IT TURNED OUT GOING to Haven's house was exactly what Shaw needed. From the moment they walked through the door, the pressure eased in his chest. His smiles turned genuine. The knots left his shoulders. By two hours in, they were in their pjs and eating cookies like they were five and it wasn't lunchtime. Joesph visibly swung between relaxed and embarrassed. Shaw couldn't look away. It was almost a relief when Joesph disappeared inside the bathroom, giving his heart a rest.

"Thank you for bringing him to me. I don't get to see him often any longer and never for long. You somehow talked him into staying a few days."

Shaw couldn't let Haven think it was him. "Actually, he brought me to you. I had a falling out with my dad this morning. We're in hiding while I decide what to do. Plus, he knew I needed to be reminded good parents exist."

Haven's expression changed. At the kitchen table where they sat, she moved her chair closer and set her hand on his forearm. Her blue eyes were a mirror image of Joesph's, making her even harder to resist. "What happened?"

As much as Shaw didn't want to talk about it, he was enraged and didn't know what to do. "I noticed our secretary has been skimming off the books. So I went to Dad to see how he wanted me to handle things. Turns out, he knew all along. It was his way of keeping their affair quiet."

Haven's shoulders fell. "Oh no." She chewed her bottom lip for a second, as if biting back all the words. They obviously beat her. "What a bastard. I hope you plan to let your mom know. If it were me, I'd definitely want to know so I could take him for everything. Plus, if she finds out and then learns you knew and didn't tell her, she'll never forgive you."

"Yeah. That's what I figured." Unfortunately, it wasn't that simple. "No matter what I do, I'll lose. If I stay quiet, I could lose my mom. If I say anything, I'll definitely lose my dad, job, and Joesph's job."

"I've already told you not to worry about me," Joesph said, returning from the bathroom. He sat. "Don't factor me at all. Just focus on what your heart tells you to do."

Exasperated didn't begin to cover his feelings. "Of course I have to consider you. You can't take less money somewhere else. In fact, you deserve more than you make now."

Haven patted his arm. "You'll do what's right. I'll let you two figure it out." She walked away, leaving them alone in the kitchen.

They waited until she was gone.

Joesph jumped in first. "Look, I won't be in any less debt by taking less money. In fact, I might finally qualify for bankruptcy. That won't clear my student loans, but at least I'll be out from underneath my medical bills. Don't worry about me."

"You still have student loans?" Shaw had no idea why that was what popped out.

"Yes. Do you have any idea how much it costs to go to law school? I didn't have parents paying my way." Joesph looked ready to bite off his own tongue. "Sorry. I didn't mean to sound so bitter."

He was right to be bitter. It was ridiculous for him to still owe money on the degree needed to work. That was nuts. "Let me know how much it is and I'll pay it off. That's something Dad should've done when he hired you. It pisses me off that he didn't."

Joesph looked beyond frustrated. "Stop. We're supposed to be talking about you. I don't want your money."

Aggravation made Shaw's decision for him. "We are talking about me. I'm starting my own firm. You're my first hire. As part of your sign-on bonus, I'll cover any student loans." The bravado left him as soon as the words did. "That is, if you trust me to make a go of things without Dad's backing. It's possible our clients won't follow me."

A bright smile exploded across Joesph's face. "They'll follow you and so will I. There's no one better than you. In fact, let's ease your mind now and put you out of your misery." Joesph grabbed his phone, turned it on, and clicked around. He left it face up and put it on speaker as ringing filled the air.

"You've reached the residence of His Royal Highness, Prince Noir. How may I direct your call?"

"This is Joesph Drake from Howe's Law firm. Is Noir available? I have business."

"Hold, please."

Elevator music filled the air, proving it was likely a service that handled his calls. Prince Noir was the firm's biggest client. All Shaw's clients were based on Noir because Noir was *the* drug lord of Atlantic City. His lackeys relied on Shaw to keep them out of prison. If Noir didn't want to leave Shaw's father's practice, this venture was dead in the water before it began. Shaw wanted to beg Joesph to hang up. He thought he might be sick.

"This is Noir." Noir sounded like the foreign prince he was.

"Hey, Noir. It's Joesph."

Noir's tone changed, turning friendly. "It's good to hear your voice. You weren't at Salem's last party. We were forced to play Two Dares a player short."

Hope slammed into Shaw. He had forgotten Noir and Joesph were actual friends. He also really wanted to know what Two Dares was.

"Yeah. I was in the hospital."

Shaw's gaze snapped to Joesph's face and didn't budge. Haven had told him Joesph had been hospitalized a couple of months back. He didn't realize he had also been hospitalized as little as a month ago. Joesph had been back working at the firm then. How had Shaw not known?

Joesph kept talking, speeding right past the topic. "I'll be there next time. So, I just wanted to give you a quick heads-up. Shaw and I will be splitting away from Howe's Law firm and becoming a separate practice. I wanted to make sure your people know where to call from now on."

Damn. He was smooth.

"Of course. I assume we'll call you directly?"

"Please? I imagine Shaw Sr. will close up shop soon, since he's retired. The good news is, prices will go down since it turns out Senior's secretary has been overcharging clients so she could keep the extra money."

Shaw covered his mouth. He wanted to laugh, but he couldn't. Joesph was so much more of everything than him, especially when it came to bravery.

"Is that so? Well, I'll definitely leave that mess for Shaw to deal with, but there's no sense in charging less. I'd have to call my accountant to tell him about the change, and it's worth the extra money to me to avoid doing that. He's very tiresome."

Shaw had to bite his lip to keep from laughing. Plus, giddiness just owned him. This was really happening. Shaw would be free.

"Okay. I'll let Shaw know. You know you can count on him."

"Always. I only hire the best. That includes you." The surety in Noir's voice had Shaw's throat swelling. He had always been the one to defend Noir and his bunch. His father had already retired before they landed him as a client. But he had needed exactly this today and Joesph had given it to him. The truth hit him so hard, it stole his breath and made him wonder why he couldn't see it before. Joesph loved him. There was no other reason he would constantly put up with Shaw and still be this amazing afterward. More than that, though. Shaw loved him too. His refusal to accept that truth was one reason his mental health had taken such a steep decline. Shaw had been so fucking determined to hang on to his freedom. He had destroyed everything, including himself. He was such a dumbass, and he didn't deserve Joesph.

Joesph offered to go with Shaw to tell his mom everything. Shaw had refused. The moment was too personal. While he knew Shaw wanted him at his side, Shaw didn't want his mom feeling any more humiliated than she already would. He asked her to meet him at the office so he could show her proof while also avoiding his dad. They could go home now, Joesph supposed, but Shaw had shot that down. He had begged Joesph to stay put and wait. So that was what Joesph did. In his mom's guest room, sitting on the bed, he chewed the side of his nail and waited. Shaw had been gone for hours. Joesph felt sick. The what ifs ate him. What if Senior found out Portia planned to meet with Shaw? What if he was already waiting when Shaw got to the office? It was crazy, but what if Shaw got hurt? His mind wanted to shy away from the thought. But what if Shaw had gotten what he wanted out of Joesph with that call to Noir and now they were done again? Obviously, they had never been more than friends, but their relationship was still very much on and off again. Damnit. As much as Joesph hated to admit it, he really wanted to join Shaw on this new venture. All Senior's clients would follow Shaw. He didn't think he would make less, even if he had to work more. Plus, it wasn't uncommon for firms to pay off student loans as part of their sign-on package. Joesph would be halfway out of debt. Even if things didn't work out, Joesph could file bankruptcy and be out from underneath everything with that loan gone. No matter what, he would be better off. He hated the way his thoughts had turned selfish, but if Senior somehow convinced Shaw to stay, Joesph would be fucked because he would definitely be out of the job. He had already checked his messages. Senior had fired him. Joesph had to think negatively about Shaw's plans. Life never gave him a reason to feel otherwise.

The bedroom door opened. Joesph's head shot up. His gaze locked on Shaw. His heart did some crazy flip thing that took away his breath. He was there. Shaw had come back.

"Hey. How'd it go?"

Shaw closed the door behind him and crossed the room. His face was set in hard lines as he climbed onto the bed. Before Joesph had time to guess at his intentions, Shaw yanked him beneath him. His mouth covered Joesph's and Joesph surrendered. There was no other way to describe what happened to his body. It knew what Shaw could do for it and cared not at all what would happen to his heart. His entire body melted, and he met Shaw, desperate, stroke for stroke. Their tongues battled as Shaw pushed Joesph's shirt up and massaged his bare skin. Joesph was lost. He wouldn't tell Shaw to stop. Joesph had known when he brought Shaw here, they would share a bed. He had known he would end up like this and he wanted it so fucking bad.

"Tell me no before I wreck you again." Shaw's words were a plea between kisses. Joesph heard the despair behind each one and he couldn't give Shaw what he wanted. Joesph needed this.

"Please don't stop."

Joesph's pajama pants were ripped down his legs. "You're an idiot."

"I know." He could hate himself later. No one else touched him. He wanted to be touched.

Shaw peeled off his shirt.

Joesph enjoyed the show. He was just so perfect and sleek. Beautiful. Everything about him was out of Joesph's league for a million reasons. He would give in every time.

Shaw kissed Joesph's stomach and then swallowed his dick. Joesph held on to the covers and bit his bottom lip. They were at his mom's house. While she wouldn't listen at doors, he couldn't be loud. In between licks and sucks, Shaw pulled a condom and packet of lube from his wallet before the wallet went sailing across the room.

A laugh burst from Joesph. "You'll be picking up credit cards for days."

"I don't care." He sounded and looked impatient.

Joesph wanted to pat himself on the back, and he didn't know why. He hadn't done anything to get Shaw hot. Truthfully, his health made him a bit useless at sex. Shaw would definitely do all the work, but he already knew that and still came back to Joesph. Joesph got the feeling Shaw preferred being in complete control. That fit his personality.

Wet fingers stretched his asshole, stealing his every thought. Shaw's tongue was in his mouth again and Joesph was a mess. He was on the verge of begging when Shaw impaled him. Shaw swallowed his cries as he gave Joesph time to adjust. The moment Joesph's muscles relaxed, Shaw rocked against him. He was hyperaware of every squeak and creak the bed made. It seemed Shaw was too. He made love to Joesph, soft and slow. That wasn't Shaw. Shaw was a plunderer. He always wrecked Joesph in every way. This was different. The way he took Joesph was more dangerous to his heart than anything Shaw had ever done. Shaw held his stare.

Joesph's eyes burned. He wanted to believe it was love that stared at him, but he knew better. Shaw would never love him. Joesph couldn't entertain those thoughts. He might not survive the next heartache if he pretended they were more.

"I don't want you to be with anyone else."

Despite the way his body burned, a bark of laughter still burst from Joesph. "You're good. Nobody else wants me."

Shaw's intensity didn't ebb. "That's not true, and you're not hearing me. I want you to be mine." He went still, making Joesph want to cry. His body had definitely been close to the edge. Shaw's actions stole his building orgasm. "We're more than friends. I just didn't want to admit it and give up being free."

"I know." He also hated Shaw a little for saying that while inside him. But Shaw's full meaning slowly penetrated the fog of his lust.

"What are you saying? That you want to be a couple—like, officially?"

"Yes."

Holy shit. Joesph could barely breathe. "Do you plan to be with just me, or am I still supposed to act like you're not killing me every time you choose someone else?"

"I've always been just yours. Like I said, I just didn't want to admit it. But you don't have to worry, there won't be anyone else."

Joesph was blown away. Shaw was buried to the hilt inside him and still managed the most important conversation of Joesph's life. "No lunches? Late night dinners? No chasing billionaires just because you can?"

"I'm sorry I ever did those things. You've always scared the hell out of me. No one sees me as clearly as you do and still cares. You're the only person who makes me want to be better. There's nothing that makes me happier than taking care of you. It's always been that way. I've just been too selfish to do what was right by you. That's over. I need to know you're really mine."

Goddamn. Joesph thought he might cry. "Okay." His voice broke.

Shaw slowly lowered his head and swiped his lips across Joesph's mouth. "I swear. This one time, you won't regret me. I just need one more chance. I promise I won't be the monster in your story this time."

A tear slipped back into Joesph's hair. His emotions were out of his control. Shaw said everything Joesph had begged the universe to hear, except for the three little words he wouldn't get. Joesph knew Shaw would never love him. That was okay. This was more than he expected to have. It didn't take long for Shaw to make him forget his own name, much less their conversation. Fuck. The guy had talent. While Shaw still moved slowly, he hit at the perfect angle. Joesph held his breath. His muscles clenched. Pressure climbed his shaft. A whimper escaped him.

"Give it to me."

At Shaw's demand, Joesph flew to pieces. He gasped for air as his body jerked. Joesph swore time stopped while pleasure rocked his soul. Then Shaw claimed his mouth and muffled cries vibrated against his lips. Joesph saw heaven. He was there with Shaw.

CHAPTER SIX

SHAW WAS AT PEACE in a way he hadn't been for a while. He was way too fucking tall for the bathtub inside Haven's house. That didn't stop him from sitting in the hot, bubbly water with Joesph between his knees. It had been a long time since they made love. He knew Joesph had to be sore. Shaw just wanted to take care of him. He loved the way Joesph felt, relaxing against his chest. Shaw never got enough of holding him.

"I texted you on my way here to see if you needed anything. You didn't respond."

"Shit. When I turned my phone back on earlier, I turned my ringer off." A soft chuckle rumbled from Joesph. "I spent hours fretting over not hearing from you, and it was my fault."

He kissed Joesph's shoulder. "It's probably for the best you kept your notifications off. Mom and I spent hours making copies of everything. I'm keeping one set and she's taking the rest home to confront Dad. There's no telling how he'll react afterward, but I know he'll blame everyone but himself."

"How did she take it? Don't answer that. That was a ridiculous question. I can't even imagine. They've been married forever."

"Almost fifty years, since a month after she turned eighteen. She wasn't as surprised as I expected. It seems Kayla isn't the first."

"Damn."

Shaw couldn't stop kissing Joesph's shoulder. He was the only comfort Shaw had. "I know. I never saw my dad as a cheater. That's crazy, I guess. We represent some of the biggest criminals in town. I guess I should've guessed he has no scruples."

"You have scruples and you're the one actually doing the defending. Someone has to."

"I guess."

Joesph snuggled closer. "You sound so sad. I hate that. Tell me how to make it better."

"You are just by being here. No one else shows up for me."

"Not that you make it easy." The laughter lacing Joesph's claim took some sting from the words. He knew it was true.

"I don't know why I'm this way."

"You were raised to believe the only people deserving of attention were the best of the best. Being perfect and right topped kindness and empathy. In fact, I imagine those things were considered a weakness in your house."

Shaw's lips found Joesph's shoulder again. Kissing him was the only peace he found. "Damn. I should've just hired you to be my therapist."

"I'm probably cheaper." He toyed with Shaw's fingers. "But I'm not an expert in that field. I just see you clearly because I haven't looked away in years."

Shaw wanted to tell Joesph a million things. He didn't know where to start. The thing was, life had always been all about him when it came to them. He had to stop. "Speaking of experts in their fields. There's a doctor in NYC that is the leading MS expert in the U.S., supposedly. Would you see him if I set up an appointment?"

"You've been talking to my mom."

Shaw wouldn't deny it. "You don't talk to me. Not really. I had to talk to someone."

For a moment, Joesph continued focusing on their hands before he finally spoke. "I've seen that guy. All the experts in the world won't change anything. I'm just one of the unlucky twenty percent of people with this disease who live in constant pain and need assistance walking. All anyone can do for me is keep trying medicines until they find something that works the best. This won't kill me, but it'll make sure I'm miserable."

Shaw's chest hurt. Joesph's issues made Shaw's problems seem trivial and self-centered. "Damn." He pressed his lips against Joesph's temple. "I'm sorry, baby. You make me feel ridiculous for my week of in-patient treatment for suicidal tendencies. What in the hell do I have to be sad about?"

Joesph moved so fast, Shaw didn't see it coming. He turned and straddled Shaw. His gaze moved over Shaw's face. "What? When did this happen? Why didn't you call me?"

Sometimes, Shaw felt so close to Joesph, he forgot there were things he hadn't said. This was one of those things. "Not long after you quit."

He watched Joesph deflate. "I know I told you to lose my number, but surely you knew I'd be there."

A sad smile tugged at his lips. "Yeah. That's the problem, isn't it? You show up for me time and time again while I fail you each and every time. I didn't want to be that guy. I didn't want to be anything anymore." Fuck. He hated admitting that out loud. It was Joesph. He was the only person Shaw trusted.

"And now?"

The hurt in Joesph's eyes had Shaw tightening his hold and pulling him closer. "Now I just want to be with you. I want the peace and happiness you bring me. But if I had showed up at your door and didn't get help, you would've gotten the same guy you've been dealing with for years. I don't want to be him anymore. It was past time to deal with my bullshit."

"I still would've been there."

A smile exploded across Shaw's face at the petulance in Joesph's tone. "You're amazing and perfect." He stole a kiss. "And beautiful and sexy." Shaw teased Joesph's lips apart. Their tongues met and stroked. Everything fell away. It hit

Shaw. He was fine. In fact, he was great. All he really needed was Joesph. Even if he had lost his clientele and his dad had probably disowned him, Shaw didn't need their money anyhow. He had been winning big for a lot of important people for several years. He was good. Shaw had Joesph. He didn't need anything else.

Joesph hated the way Shaw could distract him with his kisses. He was so mad at Shaw for not coming to him with his problems, even though he understood why he hadn't. It also warmed his heart knowing Shaw wanted to better himself so he could be who Joesph needed.

Joesph had always known this was who Shaw was behind the facade his father had forced him to create. That was why he hadn't let go.

Shaw stood and carried Joesph from the tub. He sat him on the edge and gently dried him. Joesph couldn't look away from Shaw's face. He cared. Genuinely. It was in his eyes. Joesph's throat swelled. He wanted this life with Shaw. No one could know how much.

Once dried, Shaw held out his hand. "Come on. Let's go cuddle. I've missed the hell out of that."

Joesph couldn't help his idiotic smile. That had been what he missed the most too. It was hard being invisible, and that was exactly what he was since his life changed. No one saw him any longer. Shaw treated him like nothing had changed. It was addicting.

He climbed into bed and Shaw followed. In no time, they were beneath the covers and Joesph was in Shaw's arms. He couldn't stop toying with the line of hair that ran from his navel down. Joesph knew he probably drove Shaw crazy with his inability to be still. He had just missed Shaw so much.

"What should we call the new office?"

"Hmm." Joesph welcomed any topic that stopped him from molesting Shaw. "The Law Office of Howe Jr.?"

"I was thinking Drake and Drake."

Joesph's brow furrowed. "Why would you add my name once, much less twice?"

Shaw never stopped trailing his fingertips up and down the back of Joesph's arm. "I'm adding your name because the practice is half yours. It's twice because I think I'd rather take your last name than keep mine."

Joesph shot up onto his elbow so he could meet Shaw's stare. "What?"

A sweet smile hovered on Shaw's lips. "It's okay if you want to say no."

First off, Shaw's eyes said it wasn't okay. Second, what the fuck? "Say no to what?" He would not assume a damn thing. Assuming things with Shaw broke hearts.

"Will you marry me?"

Joesph was so stunned, all he could do was blink. Never in a million damn years did he see this coming. He couldn't help but argue, because surely Shaw didn't mean it. "But you don't even love me. Is this about your dad?"

Shaw's brow furrowed. "Why would this be about my dad? And I absolutely love you. You should—" Shaw blinked a few times. "I started to say you should know that, but I guess I've never given you a reason." Fuck. He looked so defeated. A sad smile touched his lips and fell away. "I guess The Law Office of Howe Jr., it is."

"Drake and Drake is better. It's shorter on a business card."

Shaw looked scared to hope. "Are you being serious? You'll actually marry me?"

Joesph shrugged. "I mean, I love you and you're the only man I want. Why would I say no? Plus, I really can't let Dodge get two husbands before I even have one."

A bark of laughter burst from Shaw. "What does that have to do with anything?"

Joesph shrugged again. "I don't know. It's just nervous chatter, really. I keep expecting you to take it back and shut me out again."

Shaw snagged Joesph's waist and rolled, tucking him beneath him. "Never." His mouth covered Joesph's and their fingers linked. Joesph's heart soared. He had no idea if this would go anywhere. Maybe Shaw would find a new level of breaking him. It seemed he would find out because Joesph had no plans to back down. He would take this as far as Shaw went. God help them both.

CHAPTER SEVEN

GLASSES AND SILVERWARE CLINKED alongside the murmur of several voices. Bigstock Brewhouse was one of the most popular restaurants in town and was always busy at lunchtime. The moment they had a table, Shaw pulled his chair so close to Joesph's their arms brushed. Joesph hadn't stopped smiling in the two weeks since they had gotten engaged. Shaw had bought him a gorgeous engagement ring and—as promised—paid off his student loans. Joesph still felt a little weird about that part, but they were getting married. Soon that debt would be his too. A detail Shaw had pointed out several times, making Joesph feel a little better about the situation.

Shaw leaned his way with his iPad. "Okay. Big decision here. Which of these business cards do you like? The black and gold or plain white?"

Joesph's gaze slid between the two. "Honestly? It might seem a little pretentious, but our names look really good in gold."

A sexy chuckle rumbled from Shaw. Joesph had to take a breath at the sound. He was so in love. "Black it is." He scrolled. "Now, even bigger decision. Which of these wedding invitations?"

Giddiness poured through Joesph. He couldn't believe Shaw had spent the morning putting together an actual invitation. Joesph read the two choices. "This weekend?"

Shaw shrugged. "You said we have to beat Dodge to the altar. We're running out of time on that one."

They were, and Joesph hadn't been serious. "If you want to wait, we can. I'm not trying to rush you."

Shaw met and held his gaze. "You're not. I'm rushing you before you come to your senses."

Joesph tore his gaze away and focused on the invitation again. "What's this address?"

"It's a small chapel at a gorgeous winery. They were the only people with an opening. I figured, since we don't have many people to invite, we didn't need a huge place anyway. Hopefully, it's okay. I wanted to surprise you. Plus, I know you don't need the stress."

That was true. Any amount of stress caused flares, and Joesph already suffered more than he liked. "Sounds great. Who are we inviting?"

Shaw pulled up a list, proving exactly how hard he had been working on planning. "I figured Dodge's bunch, since he's your best friend."

Joesph cut in. "You're my best friend. I thought we had that established."

That goddamn sexy chuckle nearly took him out again. "Okay. Best friend you're not sleeping with."

"I'll accept this compromise."

They shared a smile before going back to the list. "We have to invite Noir and his husband."

"Along with an entire royal guard," Joesph added.

"Yep. Along with them. Your mom. That's a given."

"Your parents."

Shaw didn't say anything. He kept moving along, naming clients they also considered friends.

Joesph eyed the list. He saw Portland and Tarek as well as another couple Shaw played pickleball with at the club. His parents weren't on the list. "Hold up. Are you not inviting your parents?"

"I'd rather not."

"Not even your mom?" Joesph was so confused. He knew they had fallen out, obviously, but not inviting them to his wedding seemed a bit much.

Shaw met his stare. His eyes swam with laughter, but it felt fake. "Baby, my mom would totally take over everything. We'd end up waiting a year while she put together a gala. Plus, Dad fired you."

Joesph shrugged. "And? I planned to quit anyhow."

"It's the principle."

Sometimes, Shaw aggravated the hell out of him. But this wasn't his fight, and Shaw would do what he wanted. "Will these invitations even arrive on time? Much less have time to be sent out?"

Shaw draped his arm across the back of Joesph's chair and kissed his temple. "Don't worry, baby. I have everything under control. You can trust me."

"I know."

Shaw kissed him again at the admission.

Joesph smiled so big, it hurt. It fell the second he noticed a familiar set of eyes focused on him. "Oh, no." The words were out before Joesph could call them back. He regretted it the second he drew attention to the staring contest.

Shaw picked up his water glass and took a drink as if his father wasn't sitting across the room with the same woman who broke up his marriage.

"Why isn't she in jail?"

"Dad would have to press charges, and he won't. If I tried, Dad would just defend her in court and I doubt I could win, considering it was his business first and he basically gave her permission. So, fuck it. It's whatever."

Despite his nonchalant tone, Joesph saw the hurt in his eyes. His dad had betrayed his entire family. Joesph focused on the menu while he kept up his side of the conversation. "Why is he staring death daggers at me?"

Shaw took his hand and brought it to his mouth. He smiled as he kissed the back. "You are woefully blind to your worth. It's your dedication and hard work that made the firm a success. You were the one who stayed late and ran themself into the ground. I'm sure he feels like you chose your side and now you'll take us to the top. Mostly, it's because you stole his clients." He laughed, doing nothing to quell Joesph's irritation.

"They were our clients, and of course I chose a side. You're mine. I love you. Why would I choose a cheating old man?"

"Because this cheating old man gave you a job when no one else would have."

Joesph startled at the sudden appearance of Shaw's dad. He wanted to be embarrassed since he was right. Not only had Senior given him his first job right out of law school, but he had also taken Joesph's side against his own son more than once. Now that he really looked at things, though, what a shitty thing to do. He should've known by that act alone Senior had no loyalty.

Joesph held his stare and refused to respond.

Senior sighed as if annoyed by Joesph. "I'd like to speak to my son alone."

Where in the fuck did he want Joesph to go? They were in a restaurant.

Shaw set his hand on his arm. "Feel free to speak in front of Joesph. Obviously, he knows everything. Plus, we're getting married, so he'll be family."

Senior's face screwed up in confusion. He glanced between them. "Why? You've always only used him for sex. Why would you marry a cripple?"

Joesph's eyebrows shot up.

Shaw brushed his shoulder, snagging his attention. His face looked hard enough to cut glass. "You should go say hi to Kayla. Maybe mention how Dad spent last night begging my mom to take him back. Mom has proof if she'd like to see it."

Senior waved his hand. "You can stay. I shouldn't have said that."

Joesph didn't know what to do. On one hand, Joesph had called the guy an old cheat, so maybe they were even. But on the other, fuck this guy who chose an affair partner over his family. Thankfully, he ended up rescued.

"Hey. I thought I saw you sitting over here."

Relief poured through Joesph at Dodge's sudden appearance. His men, Salem and Quest, sat at a table nearby.

"Hey." Joesph grabbed the iPad and focused on Shaw. "I'm going to go say hi and show them what we were just talking about."

Shaw gave him a sharp nod, but his hard gaze never wavered from his father.

Joesph didn't hesitate to back away from the table and leave with Dodge.

Dodge looked confused. "What's going on? Why does Shaw look ready to kill his dad?"

"Oh, boy. It's been a wild couple of weeks." They reached the table before he could explain. Salem and Quest were all smiles.

They exchanged a round of pleasantries before Joesph jumped in, answering Dodge's question. "Very long story short,

Shaw Sr. has been cheating on his wife with his old secretary. Now Shaw and his dad are fighting and it's a mess."

Salem nodded. He always looked too serious. But Joesph had no idea what it took to be him. Salem had married a ninety-year-old billionaire months before the man's death. The guy had left Salem everything. Now Salem planned to marry the guy's stepsons. It was wild and the talk of the town. Everyone thought Salem was nothing more than a gold digger. That wasn't true. Joesph loved these men. The three were made for each other.

"I'm not surprised," Salem said, cutting into his thoughts. "J.D. used to tell me all about Shaw Sr.'s exploits. There was nothing J.D. hated more than a cheat."

That caught Joesph off guard. "Really? Shaw's mom said it wasn't the first time, but I didn't know it was all the time."

Salem nodded again. "Apparently. I'm surprised Shaw didn't know. It didn't seem like he was very discreet."

"Shaw's too fucking self-absorbed to see shit." Quest muttered the words under his breath, but Joesph didn't miss them. Joesph didn't correct him. Quest was owed his reasons to dislike Shaw.

"Anyhow, his dad just let Shaw know how he felt about his son marrying a cripple. So, can I sit with you?"

A deep line appeared between Dodge's eyebrows. "Who is Shaw marrying? I thought you two were back together."

A laugh burst from Joesph. He adored Dodge's sweet mind. "He meant me, angel."

"What? Why would he call you that? Do I need to kick his ass?"

"Congratulations." Salem sounded genuine and not at all bothered Dodge wanted to fight an old man.

"You can come live with us if anything goes wrong," Quest cut in.

Joesph shook his head. "Thanks, guys." Genuinely, Quest wasn't wrong to feel that way. Shaw had never done Joesph right in the past. This time was different, though. He felt that in his gut.

The iPad made a sound, reminding Joesph he held it. He quickly typed in Shaw's password. As he did so, it truly washed over him how much he knew about the guy. They had been much deeper in each other's lives than either of them wanted to admit. Joesph blinked at the device.

"I heard you put out feelers for a wedding venue. Surely, you're not planning to marry that cripple. Not only is he beneath you, but you'll end up taking care of him full time once he's bedridden. You should come warm my bed instead."

Joesph had no idea who the message was from. He was too hurt and angry to care. Why in the hell was everyone calling him a cripple today? Like, what the fuck? He almost would prefer if they called him the F slur. Goddamn. His chest hurt.

Dodge touched his arm. "Are you okay?"

Joesph tried for a smile. Dodge had the sweetest eyes. They almost broke Joesph. It was obvious he cared, and goddamn it. Shaw was above him and he would have to take care of Joesph. He shouldn't have agreed to this marriage. Joesph didn't want to ruin Shaw's life. With his brain numb, he simply handed the iPad to Dodge. "It's Shaw's." That was all he could say.

Dodge's expression snapped closed. He passed the iPad back. "Don't worry about that person. It's only how Shaw reacts that should matter to you. Seriously. People hit on me all the time. It would crush me if Salem or Quest blamed me for it. Just hold out and see what he says."

Joesph quickly checked over his shoulder. Shaw's dad was gone and Shaw looked at his phone. The angry scowl he had taken on while dealing with his father was still in place. He watched Shaw type.

Joesph's gaze immediately dropped to the iPad as Shaw's message came through.

"Get fucked. Don't contact me again."

Joesph bit his bottom lip. This time would be different. He believed in them.

Shaw appeared over his shoulder. "Is it okay if we eat with you? Dad will be less likely to interrupt again with an audience."

Everyone immediately rearranged their chairs to make room.

As soon as Shaw was settled, he draped his arm across the back of Joesph's chair. "Did Joesph tell you the good news?"

Joesph's face hurt from smiling. He prayed he wasn't wrong. If Shaw woke up one day and resented him, it would kill Joesph. Right now, though, he was the happiest man alive. He couldn't picture a day without Shaw.

It had been a full damn day, and it wasn't even two yet. After lunch, they drove from building to building, checking out possible office spaces with their real-tor. Joesph kept swapping between happy and looking lost in thought. Those thoughts looked sad, and Shaw felt a little sick. Dealing with his dad had mentally drained him. He couldn't deal with anything else bad today.

After their fourth location, Shaw couldn't take it anymore. He pulled Joesph aside. "What's wrong? Are you regretting me?"

Joesph's face screwed up in confusion. "Of course not. Why would you ask that?"

Shaw didn't know how to explain. He made a wild motion. "You just keep getting this look about you and I can't figure out what I've done wrong."

"I'm sorry, baby." He stroked Shaw's arm. "It's not you." Joesph hesitated. "Have you considered that you might end up caring for me full time one of these days?"

Fuck. He had seen that message. Shaw had hoped Joesph had been too busy talking to Dodge that he missed it. Shaw went down on his haunches and held Joesph's stare. "Have you considered you might have to take care of me full time someday? I could have a stroke. A heart attack. Anything. You know life doesn't give a fuck how healthy you are. Anyone can get stricken down at any moment. I want to grow old with you. Do you know what that entails? Growing old."

Joesph looked serious as he held on to every word. "There's nothing that could happen to you that I wouldn't be there with you for every step. I love you."

Shaw gave him a sharp nod. "Exactly. That's how I feel too. I'm not being rash. This isn't me blindly rushing in. You've been the biggest part of me for years. Long before this wheelchair, you were mine. You'll still be mine, no matter what happens from here. I need you to know that."

Joesph nodded.

Shaw straightened. "Now, have you liked a single one of these office spaces?"

A smile exploded across Joesph's face. "No. Am I being too picky?"

Shaw glanced around. "No. There's just something..." He turned in a circle. "Maybe we should be looking at houses instead. We can find a place that has a home office. There's no one we represent I wouldn't let come to our house."

When he focused on Joesph again, Joesph wore a huge smile. "You really want to buy a house together?"

Sometimes Joesph confused the fuck out him. "We're getting married. You know that means we share everything now, right?"

Joesph laughed. "I know. It just feels so real when you talk about *our* house."

"It is real." He didn't know what Joesph wasn't getting about this. Shaw had chosen them. He had finally figured out why he was miserable, and now he wouldn't let go.

"It'll have to be wheelchair friendly."

"Of course. Matt gave me like twenty office buildings to look at with the crazy parameters I gave him for offices. I'm sure he won't have any trouble switching to houses. There's probably way more of those."

"I love you so fucking much. You know that, right? I'd choose you every time or there'd be no one."

Shaw's throat swelled. After his father's anger and feeling like his dad chose a woman over him, Joesph had no idea how badly Shaw needed to hear he would be first. "You know I'm not like him, right?" Even Shaw heard the way his voice cracked. He cleared his throat. "I know I've fucked up a lot and I haven't given you much reason to believe in me, but I'd always choose you too."

"I believe in you. You never would've dared breathe a word about marriage if you weren't dead serious. That's who you are. You're unapologetically honest."

Shaw nodded. His throat felt a little tight. Joesph had only talked about the way

Shaw told things like they were, which wasn't always a good trait. It was obvious Shaw was failing at showing he loved Joesph too much to hurt him. It got a little harder to breathe. He wasn't sure why. Shaw sort of needed to sit down and put his head between his knees.

Joesph's expression changed. He quickly kicked up the foot rests on his chair and used his cane to stand. "What's wrong?"

Shaw tried to take a breath, and nothing happened.

Joesph pulled him toward his wheelchair. "Sit. I'm calling nine one one."

Shaw wanted to ask him not to do that. He definitely wanted to refuse to take Joesph's chair. Joesph couldn't stand for long and it was Shaw's job to take care of him. But everything went a little dark around the edges and Shaw couldn't draw a deep enough breath to say a thing. He couldn't pass out on Joesph. Joesph needed him. In a distant sort of way, he heard Joesph talking, but nothing made sense. It was like no oxygen reached his brain. A terrifying thought hit. Maybe that unexpected heart attack came sooner than he thought. Damn. He really didn't want to leave this world without Joesph as his husband where he would be protected by Shaw's money. It seemed Shaw was doomed to fail him.

CHAPTER EIGHT

JOESPH FELT SO FUCKING sick. He wanted to pace, but his body wouldn't let him. His knees shook. He was only Shaw's fiancé, so no one told him shit. Shaw just sat in the ER waiting room and lost his goddamn mind. He felt like he should do something, but he didn't know what. Shaw would lose his shit if Joesph called his parents. He didn't want to bother Dodge just to have someone sit with him. Joesph only had his cane because it was too much to drag out his wheelchair. His arms felt weak as hell with the stress wearing him down. Hours passed, and he could barely hold up his head. But Joesph's spine was steel because Shaw was right. It was their job to take care of each other. That was nonnegotiable.

Six hours in, Joesph had caved and asked to go back. Unfortunately, he was reminded he was not family. He went back to waiting. Joesph was determined he would sit there all night, no matter the cost to his health. He wouldn't leave without Shaw.

Shaw: *Did you go home or come to the hospital?*

Joesph nearly cried in relief at the sight of Shaw's text. At least he knew his man was still alive.

Joesph: *I'm here. They won't let me come back because I'm not family. I followed the ambulance here and never left. You have no idea how relieved I am to get your text. Are you okay?*

Shaw*: I still don't really know anything. It looks like it might've been just a major panic attack. They're still waiting for some tests. I was just now allowed to leave the bed to find my phone. They have me in the red grippy socks. Give me a few. I'll make sure you can come and wait with me.*

Joesph rubbed his forehead. Red socks meant Shaw was obviously considered a fall risk. Likely they had an alarm set on the bed, ensuring he couldn't leave it. Joesph tried taking a few steadying breaths. Shaw was okay. They were making sure he stayed that way. Joesph could sit here.

Joesph: *I love you. Don't get your blood pressure up. I can sit here for as long as it takes.*

Truthfully, Joesph didn't know if that was true. He was going downhill after missing dinner and being trapped for hours with his feet on the floor. His eyelids felt heavy. The exhaustion kicked his ass.

Shaw: *I love you too. Don't worry about my blood pressure. You'd be more comfortable in a room with me. It's my job to take care of you.*

He was already in a room? More and more, this didn't sound like nothing. Shaw hadn't texted him again and Joesph didn't know how much more he could take. Before Joesph had time to open his texts again to check on him, the automatic doors opened. A furious-looking Shaw Sr. breezed inside, wearing his usual expensive suit.

He motioned for Joesph as he passed. "Let's go."

Joesph scrambled to obey. For an older man, Senior walked fast as hell. Joesph fought to keep pace with his legs swollen and his cane barely keeping him upright.

Senior stormed toward the only available nurse behind the counter. "My son-in-law has been sitting in this waiting room for well over eight hours already, with no word about his husband. He has been denied the right to sit with my son in his time of need. You and I both know this is a simple case of discrimination against a same-sex couple. Make no mistake, I've never lost a case and I will sue this hospital into bankruptcy if this isn't resolved."

Joesph was horrified.

She looked taken aback. "What's your son's name?"

"Shaw Howe."

She typed on the computer. A deep line between her eyebrows. "I'm sorry. There's no spouse listed."

Senior's spine stiffened. "Well, he obviously exists. He's standing right here. So that detail in his chart seems a bit intentional."

The obviously overworked nurse typed again. "What's your son-in-law's name? I can add him to the system, then you're both free to go back."

"Joesph."

"Same last name, I'm assuming."

Joesph panicked a little. If anyone wanted him to prove his identity, he was fucked. "It's Drake, actually. I kept my last name. Maybe that's what caused the confusion."

She flashed him a small smile. "That's probably it." She typed a little more. "Okay, it looks like your husband has already been moved to a room. Third floor. Room 305."

Joesph nodded. "Thank you."

Senior squeezed his shoulder. "There you go. Everything should be good now. If not, just call." He headed toward the door.

Joesph went after him. "Don't you want to come see him?"

Senior flashed him a sad-looking smile. "I can only make him worse. When he texted me, I knew he wouldn't have done so for any other reason than you. If I go up, he'll probably fall right back into whatever landed him here."

Joesph couldn't argue with that. "Thank you."

With a nod, Shaw Sr. headed out, leaving Joesph to find the elevator. Joesph couldn't get to Shaw fast enough. He needed to see the other half of his soul. That was all that mattered.

Shaw stared at the TV, seeing nothing. He chewed the side of his nail. A soft knock sounded on the door, making Shaw want to growl. He needed Joesph, and all he kept getting were nurses and doctors. He had been scared as hell and his mind was all over the place. It bothered him that Joesph hadn't shown. Now that he knew they had intentionally kept him away, he was fucking furious.

Joesph stuck his head in the door. Shaw nearly cried out in relief.

"Hey. Is it okay if I come in?"

"Are you joking? Get your ass in here. I knew Dad would get you in."

Joesph slipped into the room, limping worse than ever. Every step was likely torture. "He said he didn't want to come up and raise your blood pressure."

Shaw rubbed his chest. His dad and he would find their way. Maybe. One of these days. Right now, all Shaw cared about was Joesph. He looked like hell. It was Shaw's job to take care of him.

Joesph kissed him. "Stop. I don't know what you're thinking, but you're getting that same look as you had before you came here. If it's me, just say so. All I care about is your health."

Shaw's heartbeat slowed. Joesph was here. He would focus on that rather than the bad... like how he drove Joesph to the edge of death. He hadn't had these many bad thoughts since...

"Oh."

A smile exploded across Joesph's face. He pulled the chair closer to the bed so he could hold Shaw's hand. "What was that *oh* all about?"

Shaw shook his head at his own terrible memory. "I just realized I've been so busy trying to do everything that I haven't taken my meds in over a week."

"That's not good."

No. It wasn't. No wonder Shaw stayed on the edge of a meltdown. "With all the hopping between my place and yours, I forgot."

Joesph nodded. "You definitely need a steady routine. When we move in together, I'll keep you on schedule. You'd be amazed at how quickly meds can become part of your day that easily slips away. I've found some tricks."

The idea of living with Joesph full time had Shaw smiling.

"That makes sense, though," Joesph added. "The way you are right now, I mean. You're not supposed to stop those meds cold turkey. Your body is probably going through dopamine withdrawals."

Shaw made a helpless gesture. "I just started having a bunch of thoughts about how I'm failing. Once they started, they just kept snowballing and getting darker. I mean, I spent years letting you down. Why should you believe in me now?"

Joesph shrugged. "Because I do. I've studied every detail of us over the years and I don't think for a second I kept coming back because I'm desperate. It's nothing like that. I see you. This is love."

He always awed Shaw with his love and forgiveness. "No one else out there holds a candle to you."

A doctor strolled in, bouncy and chewing gum like it was the middle of the day and not the night. Light blue eyes landed on him and then quickly—almost like a double take—swung Joesph's way.

"Holy shit." He covered his mouth for half a second, as if horrified by his unprofessionalism. "Sorry. I just can't believe it's you."

Joesph pushed his way to his feet. A huge smile lit his face. The doctor met him more than halfway. They hugged. "Wow. It's so great to see you. I didn't know you lived here. What about the position at Vanderbilt?"

The guy pulled a face. "Yeah. Turns out I'm better at home."

Shaw eyed the pair. They were obviously close friends. The doctor was objectively handsome with his dark hair and light eyes. Shaw kind of wanted to punch him in his gorgeous square jaw.

He motioned toward Joesph's cane. "What's going on here?" Shaw hated how concerned he looked.

Shaw cleared his throat.

Joesph stepped back, drawing Shaw's attention to how close the pair had been standing. He motioned Shaw's way. "This is my husband, Shaw. Shaw, Dr. Kace Brightly. We went to college together."

Kace stayed focused on Joesph. "Husband? Dang. I really hoped you'd invite me to something that huge."

Joesph winced. "He's actually my fiancé, but for hospital reasons, he's my husband. The nursing station left me worrying my ass off for like nine hours. My future father-in-law had to come up here and straighten things out, so I'd be allowed to stay."

"Oh. Well. Sometimes you have to do what you have to do in our community. An unfortunate number of homophobes are feeling emboldened these days."

Great. He was gay. Shaw was here, a mental mess, and Joesph had this guy who looked at him in a way Shaw loathed.

Kace finally focused on him. "As long as you're cool with us openly talking about all your tests, then I'm good. I can't have Joesph worrying." He tossed a wink Joesph's way. Shaw immediately hated him.

Shaw would be damned if he let Joesph out of his sight around this Lothario. It was obvious they had slept together at some point. "I'm good. We're getting married this weekend."

Kace sent Joesph a laughing look. "And you acted like I hadn't been invited because you weren't married yet."

"No one's been invited yet. My number is still the same. Text me your address and I'll make sure you get an invitation."

"You're getting married this weekend and you haven't sent out invitations yet?"

Joesph shrugged. "It was a last-minute decision to have the wedding this soon, and we don't intend to invite many people. Shaw says he'll take care of everything. There's no one I trust more to do exactly that." Joesph paused. He looked worried. "Unless these tests are about to steal all of that."

Kace startled a little, as if he had forgotten he held a small laptop and was there for Shaw. Almost as if he had slowly been falling into Joesph's eyes. "Oh. Sorry. Seeing you again is just... I can't believe it."

Joesph smiled in a way he only did for Shaw.

Shaw's blood pressure shot through the roof. A machine blared.

Kace turned doctor in an instant. He eyed the machines while turning down the sound. "You see this?" He pointed at Shaw's rapid heartbeat.

"I can't breathe."

Joesph was at his side in a second.

Kace nodded. "Take a few breaths. I've ordered some medicine for you." He pointed at the screen again. "Your heart shouldn't beat that fast unless you're running a marathon. We ran all the tests and ruled out all the big stuff. I think this is a case of your heart messing up its signals. Your heart is just an electrical device, keeping you alive. If one node stops talking to another, you end up with what's called an arrhythmia. Unfortunately, in your case, you'll definitely need medication to manage it. This is a manageable thing, but you have to stick to a schedule with your meds, get plenty of exercise, and rest. More than anything, you need to cut back on stress. Manageable or not, this is still a life-changing diagnosis. You need to take it seriously. If you don't keep your heart rate in check, through everything I've listed, your heart could eventually fail. I don't say that scare you. As I said, you'll be okay if you take this seriously. But I know how men can be, since—you know—I am one. We like to think we can't be struck down. Everyone can and you have. It's time to slow down."

Shaw couldn't stop studying the guy, deciphering his every shift in his expression. While he understood he had been given a scary diagnosis, he still felt oddly relieved. It wasn't a panic attack. He didn't need to go back to inpatient treatment. This was physical. He could fight something physical. It was the mental bits that always kicked his ass. "Okay. Whatever keeps me here longer with Joesph."

Kace nodded. "Definitely. We were pretty close back in college. I wouldn't want anything to make him sad." He looked away, dismissing Shaw for Joesph. "Now, tell me about the cane."

Joesph had sat back down the moment Kace had focused on Shaw. He looked tired, and it hadn't escaped Shaw's notice how badly Joesph's hands shook. He flashed a sad smile. "MS."

A thought hit. "Did you take your meds tonight?"

"I haven't been home, baby."

"From the way your hands are shaking, either your current treatment isn't working or you're having a flare-up."

Joesph winced at Kace's words. "It's a flare. I'm fine."

It pissed Shaw off more than a little that Joesph admitted that to Kace and not him. "You shouldn't be skipping your meds right now."

A sweet look turned his way. "Don't worry about me. Get what you need and we can deal with whatever when we get home."

Home. The idea made him smile. Plus, it was obvious Joesph did everything he could to keep pointing out they were a couple. While they didn't have a home they shared yet, they never slept apart. It looked like they would tonight. He hated that.

He focused on Kace. "I know I've been admitted, but is there any chance of me going home tonight? Joesph is just stubborn enough to sit here in pain."

"Yeah. It's obvious he loves you." He spent a second typing on the computer. His gaze stayed locked on the device as he spoke. "Once your meds get here." The door opened, and a nurse strolled in. Kace barely spared her a glance. "Speak of the devil. Give it two hours and I'll be back. I'll take another look at your numbers. If you're stable and willing to pick up your new prescription on the way home, I'll release you." He focused on Joesph. "If I don't like what I see, is there anyone who can bring your meds?"

"I can call my mom."

"*Mhm*. I can't imagine Haven loving the idea of getting out this late." He checked his watch.

Shaw seethed.

"I have a break in about an hour. If you'd like, I can run and grab them."

Joesph sighed. "Why does no one trust me to take care of myself?"

"Because you won't choose to take care of yourself," Shaw said at the same time as Kace.

They flashed each other a smile. All the sudden, Shaw felt oddly okay with the guy. He obviously cared about Joesph and Shaw knew Joesph would never crush him.

Joesph shoved his way to his feet. "Fine. Great. Whatever. I'll go. You need to stay the night and make sure you're okay. Otherwise, I'll worry myself sick." He swayed on his feet.

Kace practically threw his laptop on the bed. It hit Shaw's shins, but he didn't care. His only worry was Joesph. "Whoa. Hey. You okay?"

Shaw knew the nurse pushed meds through his IV, but he didn't pay attention. He was too busy watching Joesph. Almost immediately, he felt better. His gaze slid toward the machine. His heart rate had dropped considerably. That was good, since Joesph scared the shit out of him.

"You okay, baby? Talk to me."

Joesph made a dismissive motion after falling back into his seat. "I'm fine. Just a little dizzy."

Kace went to work, checking Joesph's eyes and pulse. "You're not fine. Stop saying that."

Shaw snatched up his phone and called Haven.

She answered on the second ring like she knew he would never call this late for no reason. "What's wrong?"

"Hey, sexy lady. Sorry to call so late."

"Who is he talking to?" Kace sounded outraged on Joesph's behalf.

"My mom." There was no missing the laughter in his voice.

"Don't worry about me. What's wrong?" Haven sounded a little panicked.

"I'm in the hospital. I'm fine," he added before she could worry any more than he had already done. "But Joesph is here with me and refuses to take care of himself. He won't go home to take his meds or eat anything."

"Is he tattling on you to your mom?"

Joesph laughed. "Yeah. I think she loves him more than me."

Shaw shot him an annoyed look while Haven went into action. "Okay, I'm grabbing my keys. Don't worry about a thing. I'll swing by his house and grab everything he needs. Is there anything you need? Are they feeding you? Are you hungry?"

"No and a little, yeah."

"Okay, sweetie. I'll be there as soon as I can, but you know I'm fast." She cackled.

Despite everything, he couldn't stop smiling. "Don't get a ticket, speed racer."

"Meh. See you soon. Love you. I hope you get to feeling better. You can tell me all about it when I get there."

"Thank you. I love you too."

Haven disconnected first, and Shaw set his phone aside.

"Mom has things under control."

Kace stared at him, looking slightly confused.

Joesph shook his head, but there was no missing his smile. They held each other's stare. Everyone else disappeared. They would be fine. After all, they had each other. There was no better team.

CHAPTER NINE

IT HAD BEEN YEARS since Kace set eyes on Joesph. At one time, he had thought he would ask Joesph to marry him. Of course, life had taken a different turn when he had been offered a high-paying job at a hospital in Nashville. Kace had been forced to choose. He had chosen his career. Joesph never seemed to begrudge him that. In fact, they had tried to do the long-distance thing. That had failed miserably once those night shifts hit. Fuck. He was still sexy as hell. Kace had lain awake all night for two nights, thinking about him. Then a messenger had shown up with an invitation to Joesph's wedding. Reality truly dropped the hammer. When he had moved home from Nashville three years ago, he had thought several times about Joesph. At one point in his life, Joesph had been the greatest love of his life. Too many times to count, he almost looked him up. Several thoughts had always stopped him. What if he hated Kace for choosing a job over him? Maybe he was married. No doubt someone treated him the way he deserved. Now he headed to the man's wedding. It was surreal. He was so fucking pissed at himself. Kace had looked this Shaw guy up online. It seemed he was money come from money on top of money. Joesph deserved that life. More than that, he deserved to have a man treat him the way Kace had watched Shaw treat him. The guy had been way more worried about Joesph's health than his and he was the one in the hospital discussing his heart.

Kace pulled into the parking lot of the tiny chapel where the wedding was being held. He wanted to beat his head against the wall. This should've been his life. It should be his wedding, although Kace would like to think they'd have a nicer venue. The vineyard was pretty, but it was odd to see such a powerful and wealthy man choose this place. With a sigh, he climbed from the car. He headed for the door with his head held high. The moment he stepped inside, his curiosity flew through the roof. Prince Noir was there with a full royal guard. Everyone knew him. He was constantly on TV, fascinating the world with the wild notion of a prince living in America. It looked like he sat on Joesph's side of the chapel, since Haven sat in the front row. She turned her head and caught sight of him. A huge smile exploded across her face. Kace felt the same smile on his. She stood and met him halfway.

When they hugged, Kace fought the urge to close his eyes. She always gave the best hugs. Mom hugs. No one knew how amazing those were until they were gone.

She pulled away but held on to his hands. "It's been so long. You're even more handsome."

"And you're twice as beautiful."

She swatted his chest. "I'm so glad you came. Joesph worried you wouldn't."

"Of course. Joesph has been my friend for a long time."

"Well, more than a friend," Haven tacked on to his claim. "But I knew you'd be here."

"So." He rubbed the back of his neck. "I met Shaw briefly."

"Yeah. Joesph told me you treated Shaw at the hospital."

Kace nodded. "Are we happy about this wedding?"

Haven laughed. Her bright smile never dimmed. "I won't lie and say they haven't had hard times. Shaw's family is...well, Shaw's family. They're rich and pretentious. It's always been more important for

Shaw to be successful than loved. But he desperately loves my son. He treats him like a king and puts him first. Shaw would give up everything before he let go of Joesph."

Kace didn't miss the dig. He glanced around. "I guess I should find a seat."

Haven took his arm. "Nonsense. You'll sit with me. I want you to meet my nephew."

Kace suppressed a groan but let himself get dragged along. Damn. He hoped this wedding wasn't about to go from a bad day to a total nightmare. There was nothing he hated worse than someone playing matchmaker. It happened way more than he liked since he was a doctor. It seemed everyone suddenly had a nephew. He already felt like this was hell just because of the occasion. The idea that things couldn't get worse flew straight out the window at the sight of Jamison waiting for Haven. Time stopped. Jamison's closed expression gave away nothing. After all, it wasn't every day a man ran into the professional he hired about once a month to snuggle with him. Holy shit. This day was even worse than he could have dreamed. Not only was he humiliated, but he also had the horrible realization the guy was Joesph's cousin. He wanted to die.

There was so much happiness bubbling inside Shaw. He had been married exactly one day, and he was still riding the high. He hit his blinker.

"This isn't the way to the airport."

Shaw's permanent smile grew. "I know. We have four hours until our flight leaves. I have to make a stop." He stopped at the gate of a prestigious neighborhood a few blocks over from his house. The gate swung wide as Shaw approached, proving his new sensor worked.

"Where are we going?" Joesph looked adorably confused.

Shaw kissed his hand. "You'll see." He turned into a driveway and parked outside the three-car garage. Shaw motioned for Joesph to stay in the car. "Wait just a second."

Joesph eyed the house. "Okay."

Shaw quickly moved to the trunk and pulled out Joesph's wheelchair. He knew Joesph likely didn't need it for this. But they had a long way to go through airports, since they never put wheelchair pickup anywhere convenient. Plus, he needed Joesph to see something.

Joesph looked twice as confused when Shaw opened the door with his chair waiting. He gave Shaw a questioning look as he swapped from the car to the wheelchair. "Are you sure we'll make our flight? Whose house is this?"

Shaw huffed. "Can you wait half a second? Dang."

Joesph held his hands up in surrender. "All right. I trust you."

Appeased, Shaw steered Joesph to the door. The sidewalk was more than wide enough for the chair and there were no steps. As he unlocked the door, he saw the way Joesph fought not to ask more questions. He didn't have the luxury of silence any longer when he pushed Joesph into an empty house.

"What do you think? It's completely wheelchair accessible. You should check out the kitchen. Oh, and it has the perfect space for our home office."

Joesph spun his chair and focused on Shaw. "This is gorgeous, but we're technically on our honeymoon and you're supposed to be relaxing. Not worrying about the future."

Shaw rolled his eyes. Joesph could be too overprotective at times. "Would you go look? You'll love it."

He rolled himself from the wide foyer to the living room. He made it look effortless on the sleek wood floors that were perfect for wheelchair use. From the living room, he rolled into the kitchen. "Oh, wow. I do love it. The cabinets and countertops are all within reach."

"Good. It's your wedding gift."

Joesph spun so fast, Shaw couldn't believe he kept the chair upright. "What?"

He was more than a little proud of himself for pulling off this secret without giving himself away. "Yeah. While we worked on wedding stuff, our realtor was hard at work. I toured a few places while you were at your doctor's appointment. One wire transfer later, wedding gift."

Joesph blinked. "Like that? No closing date? You just bought a house."

One day, Joesph would realize how money moved mountains. "I'm sure plenty of things went on behind the scenes, but I wasn't needed for it. That's what lawyers are for."

A smile exploded across Joesph's face. "I love how you just said that, like we're not lawyers."

Shaw shrugged. "Even the best attorneys need representation. Only idiots represent themselves."

For a moment, Joesph simply stared at him. "But really, are you serious? This is a whole house. I can't afford to buy you a house for a wedding gift."

"First of all, I got the best gift imaginable when I got you. You gave me that. Secondly, we don't need another house. We already have two we need to sell, and now we have a third for us to share. So that gift wouldn't work for me. Third, you absolutely can afford to buy me anything. We're married. Everything is ours now."

Joesph shook his head. "I can't believe you bought me a house."

Shaw shifted from foot to foot. Joesph didn't sound like he wanted Shaw's gift. "I mean, if you don't like it, I'm sure there's something we can do."

Joesph pushed his way from his chair. "What are you talking about? I've only seen two rooms and I absolutely love it. It's from you." He made his way into Shaw's arms. "You're the most incredible guy and I don't deserve you."

Shaw blew out a raspberry. "You totally deserve me."

Joesph swiped a kiss across his lips, laughing. "I totally deserve you."

Shaw locked his arms around Joesph's waist so he couldn't get away while he took the kiss he wanted. Their wedding night had been long and strenuous. That didn't stop Shaw from going hard, like no one had touched his dick in years. His hands slid to Joesph's ass. He hauled him closer so Joesph could see what he did to Shaw. Shaw found Joesph hard for him too.

"Damn. Are you sure you want to go to Curacao? We could just stay right here. Surely there's somewhere in this huge place where I can take you down."

Joesph groaned. "Don't tempt me like that. I'm a weak man and we need this vacation. We need to walk away from everything for a while. If nothing else, our health needs us to take a break."

"But you feel so good." Shaw squeezed Joesph's ass. "I don't want to be good."

Joesph kissed his neck, making things worse. Finally, he took a step back. "We have to focus on something else. I'm really proud of you for inviting your parents to the wedding. I know how hard that was, but it was the right thing to do. One day, you three will work through this, but they would never forgive you if you had gotten married without them."

Shaw nodded along, not really hearing a thing. "It only takes fifteen minutes to get to the airport. I can easily get you off in under ten. That leaves us plenty of time to get through security."

For a moment, Shaw wondered if he angered Joesph with his inability to stay on topic, since Joesph stared at nothing, expressionless. It turned out he worked on the math in his head. "Yeah. Okay."

With all the permission he needed, Shaw had Joesph half from his clothes, his ass on the counter, and bobbed on his dick in no time. Joesph gripped the edge, looking like a dying man. "Fuck, Shaw. You weren't joking. I don't think I'll make it anywhere near ten. Play with yourself. I want to watch you come."

Nothing but happiness and pleasure lived inside Shaw. He had been so close to ending it all only a few short months earlier. There was no way he could've foreseen this future for himself. Joesph's creamy salt coating his tongue made him wonder how he ever thought he could be anywhere Joesph wasn't. He definitely couldn't have pictured himself like this during those dark days—dick in hand and about to blow on the brand-new kitchen floor of the house he would soon share with the greatest of men. One bad decision had nearly stolen this from him. Life was funny sometimes. Right now, it was perfect. It was fucking bliss.

Keep an eye out for the next Atlantic City's Most Wanted: *Exposed*.

About the Author

CHARITY PARKERSON IS AN award-winning and multi-published author with several companies. Born with no filter from her brain to her mouth, she decided to take this odd quirk and insert it in her characters. One of her greatest loves is writing morally gray characters. You'll find them scattered throughout her hundreds of titles.

*Nine-time Readers' Favorite Award Winner

*2015 Passionate Plume Award Finalist

*2013 Reviewers' Choice Award Winner

*2012 ARRA Finalist for Favorite Paranormal Romance

*Five-time winner of The Mistress of the Darkpath

Connect with her online:

*Sign up for her newsletter: https://bit.ly/charityparkersonnewsletter

*Join her readers' group on Facebook: http://bit.ly/CharitysTribe

*Website: https://www.charityparkerson.com

*A list of her social media accounts and giveaways all in one place: http://hy.page/charityparkerson